H. Irving Hancock

Dave Darrin At Vera Cruz

H. Irving Hancock

Dave Darrin At Vera Cruz

1st Edition | ISBN: 978-3-75236-110-0

Place of Publication: Frankfurt am Main, Germany

Year of Publication: 2020

Outlook Verlag GmbH, Germany.

Reproduction of the original.

DAVE DARRIN AT VERA CRUZ

Fighting with the U.S. Navy in Mexico
by

H. IRVING HANCOCK

CHAPTER I

"Do you care to go out this evening, Danny boy?" asked Dave Darrin, stepping into his chum's room.

"I'm too excited and too tired," confessed Ensign Dalzell. "The first thing I want is a hot bath, the second, pajamas, and the third, a long sleep."

"Too bad," sighed Dave. "I wanted an hour's stroll along Broadway."

"Don't let my indolence keep you in," urged Dalzell. "If you're going out, then I can have the first hot bath, and be as long about it as I please. Then I'll get into pajamas and ready for bed. By that time you'll be in and we can say 'good night' to each other."

"I feel a bit mean about quitting you," Dave murmured.

"And I feel a whole lot meaner not to go out with you," Dan promptly assured his chum. "So let's compromise; you go out and I'll stay in."

"That sounds like a very odd compromise," laughed Darrin. "On the whole, Dan, I believe I won't go out."

"If that's the way you feel," argued Dalzell, "then I'm going to change my mind and go out with you. I won't be the means of keeping you from your stroll."

"But you really don't want to go out," Dave objected.

"Candidly, I don't care much about going out; I want that bath and I'm tired. Yet in the good old cause of friendship——"

"Friendship doesn't enter in, here," Dave interposed. "Danny boy, you stay here in the hotel and have your bath, I'll go out and pay my very slight respects to Broadway. Doubtless, by the time you're in pajamas, I'll be back, and with all my longing for wandering satisfied."

"Then, if you really don't mind——"

"Not at all, old chap! So long! Back in a little while."

Through the bathroom that connected their two rooms at the Allsordia Hotel, Dave Darrin stepped into his own apartment.

Having donned coat and top-coat, Darrin picked up his new derby hat and stepped to his room door. In another half minute he was going down on the elevator. Then he stepped into the street.

Dave Darrin was young, healthy, happy, reasonably good-looking. His top-coat and gray suit were well tailored. Yet, save for his erect, military carriage, there was nothing to distinguish him from the thousands of average well-dressed young men who thronged Broadway after dark on this evening in late March.

For perhaps fifteen blocks he strolled uptown. All that he saw on that gaily lighted main thoroughfare of New York was interesting. It was the same old evening crowd, on pleasure bent.

Then, crossing over to the east side of Broadway, Dave sauntered slowly back.

Laughing girls eyed the young naval officer as he passed. Drivers of taxicabs looked the young man over speculatively, as though wondering whether he might be inveigled into going on a, to them, profitable round of New York's night sights. Human harpies, in the form of "confidence men"—-swindlers on the lookout for prey—-glanced but once at the young naval ensign, then looked away. Dave Darrin's erect carriage, his clear steady eyes, his broad shoulders and evident physical mastery of himself made these swindlers hesitate at the thought of tackling him.

Through the occasionally opened doors of the restaurants came the sounds of music and laughter, but Dave felt no desire to enter.

He was several blocks on his homeward way, and was passing the corner of a side street quieter than the others, when he heard a woman's stifled cry of alarm.

Halting, bringing his heels together with a click, and throwing his shoulders back, Darrin stopped on the corner and looked down the street.

Five or six doors away, close to a building, stood a young woman of not more than twenty-two. Though she was strikingly pretty, Dave did not note that fact in the first glance. He saw, however, that she was well dressed in the latest spring garments, and that her pose was one of retreat from the man who stood before her.

That the man had the external appearance of the gentleman was the \ first fact Darrin observed.

Then he heard the young woman's indignant utterance:

"You coward!"

"That is a taunt not often thrown at me," the young man laughed, carelessly.

"Only a coward would attempt to win a woman's love by threats," replied the girl, more calmly, though bitterness rang in her tone. "As for you, I wish to assure you that I am quite through with you!"

"Oh, no, you're not!" rejoined the annoyer, with the air of one who knows himself to be victor. "In fact, you will do very much as I wish, or your brother ——."

"You coward!" spoke the girl, scornfully again.

"If your brother suffers, your pride will be in the dust," insisted the annoyer, "and, remember, I, alone, can save your brother from disgrace."

"I am not even going to ask you to do it," retorted the young woman. "And now our interview is over. I am going to leave you, and I shall not see you again. I——."

"Going to leave me, are you?" leered her tormentor. He stepped forward, holding out his hand, as though to seize the young woman's wrist, but she alertly eluded him.

"If you try again to touch me, or if you attempt to follow me," warned the young woman, "I shall appeal for assistance."

So absorbed were the disputants in their quarrel that neither had noticed Darrin, standing on the corner.

The tormentor's face flushed, then went white, "Make your appeal," he dared, "and see what happens!"

Again he attempted to take the girl by the wrist.

"Can I be of service, madam?" inquired Darrin, as he strode toward them.

Like a flash, the annoyer wheeled upon Darrin, his eyes flashing dangerously.

"Young man," he warned, threateningly, "the best thing you can possibly do will be to make yourself scarce as quickly as possible. As for this young woman——."

The tormentor moved a step nearer to the young woman, whose face had turned very pale.

Dave slipped quietly between them.

"As this young woman does not wish to talk with you," Darrin suggested, "you may address all your remarks to me."

While the two young men stood eyeing each other Darrin noted that the young woman's annoyer was somewhat taller than himself, broader of shoulder and deeper of chest. He had the same confidence of athletic poise that Dave himself displayed. In a resort to force, it looked as though the stranger would have the better of it.

Yet this stranger seemed suddenly deprived of much of his assurance. Plainly, there was some good reason why he did not wish to fight on this side street so close to Broadway.

"Madam," inquired Darrin, half turning, "may I have the pleasure of escorting you to your friends?"

"If you will call a taxi——-" she began, eagerly.

At that moment a fareless taxicab turned the corner of Broadway and came slowly down the street.

"Hold on, chauffeur!" cried Darrin, in a voice of command. Then, as the cab stopped at the curb, Dave turned his back upon the tormentor for a moment, while he assisted the young woman into the taxicab.

"Do you feel satisfied to go without escort," asked Darrin, "or may I offer my services in seeing you safely to your home?"

"I shall be all right now," replied the young woman, the troubled look in her lustrous brown eyes vanishing as she favored her unknown defender with a smile. "If the driver will stop, two blocks from here, I will direct him where to take me."

"Step aside, boy!" ordered the unknown man, as he tried to brush Dave away and enter the cab.

It was no time for gentle measures. Ensign Darrin's right fist landed heavily on the face of the stranger, sending him prone to the sidewalk.

At a wave of Dave's hand the chauffeur started away. Scenting trouble, the chauffeur drove as fast as he could down the side street, making the round of the block, then heading into Broadway and going uptown, for the young woman had called out her destination.

As for the stranger whom Dave had knocked down, the fellow was on his feet like a flash. Ignoring Darrin, he tried to dash down the side street after the taxicab.

"Step back!" ordered Dave, catching hold of the fellow, and swinging him around. "You're not going to follow."

"I must have the number of that taxicab," cried the stranger, desperately.

"Too late," smiled Dave, as he saw the taxicab turn the next corner. "You won't learn the number. I happened to see it, though," he added incautiously.

"Give it to me, then," commanded the other. "I'll overlook what you've done if you truthfully give me the number of that taxicab. Find that girl I must, and as early as possible. Though I know her well, and her family, too, I do not know where to look for them in New York."

Dave, without a word, turned as though to walk toward Broadway.

"Give me that taxi's number," insisted the stranger.

"I won't," Dave returned, flatly.

"Give me that number, or——-"

"Or what?" drawled Darrin halting and glancing contemptuously at the furious face before him.

"Or I'll pound the number out of you!" came the ugly challenge.

"Go ahead," Dave invited, coolly. "I don't mind a fight in the least, though perhaps you would, for I see a policeman coming up the street. He would be bound to arrest both of us. Perhaps you have better reasons than I have for not courting the activities of the police."

It was plain that a fearful, even though brief struggle, took place in the stranger's mind before he made reply to Dave's taunt.

"I'll find you again, and the next time you shall not get off so easily," muttered the other. "Depend upon it, I shall see you again!"

With that the stranger walked toward Broadway. Smiling, Dave strolled more slowly after him. By the time the naval ensign reached the corner of that great artery of human life, the stranger had lost himself in the crowds of people that thronged Broadway.

"If I see him again within twenty-four hours, I think I shall know him," laughed Darrin. "My first blow put a red welt on his cheek for purposes of identification."

Then Darrin finished his walk, turning in at the Allsordia.

Dan Dalzell had also finished his bath, and lounging comfortably in his pajamas, was reading a late edition of the evening newspaper. "Have any fun?" asked Ensign Dalzell, glancing up.

"Just a little bit of a frolic," smiled Darrin, and told his chum what had happened.

"I'm glad you punched the scoundrel," flared Danny Grin.

"I couldn't do anything else," Dave answered soberly, "and if it weren't for the shame of treating a woman in such high-handed fashion as that fellow did,

I'd look upon the whole affair as a pleasant diversion."

"So he's going to look for you and find you, then settle up this night's business with you, is he?" demanded Dalzell, with one of the grins that had made him famous. "Humph! If he finds you after ten o'clock to-morrow morning, it will be aboard one of our biggest battleships and among fifteen hundred fighting men."

"I'm afraid I shall never see him again," sighed Dave. "It's too bad, too, for I'm not satisfied with the one blow that I had the pleasure of giving him. I'd like to meet the fellow in a place where I could express and fully back up my opinion of him."

"I wonder if you'll ever meet him again?" mused Dalzell, aloud.

"It's not worth wondering about," Dave returned. "I must get into my bath now. I'll be out soon."

Fifteen minutes later Darrin looked into the room, saying good night to his chum. Then he retired to his own sleeping room; five minutes later he was sound asleep.

No strangers to our readers are Dave Darrin and Dan Dalzell "Darry" and "Danny Grin," as they were known to many of their friends. As members of that famous schoolboy group known as Dick & Co. they were first encountered in the pages of the *"Grammar School Boys Series."* All our readers are familiar with the careers in sport and adventure that were achieved by those splendid Gridley boys, Dick Prescott, Dave Darrin, Greg Holmes, Dan Dalzell, Tom Reade and Harry Hazelton. The same boys, a little older and twice as daring, were again found in the pages of the *"High School Boys Series,"* and then immediately afterward in the *"High School Boys' Vacation Series."*

It was in the *"Dick Prescott Christmas Series"* that we found all six of our fine, manly young friends in the full flower of high school boyhood. A few months after that the six were separated. The further fortunes of Dick Prescott and Greg Holmes are then found in the *"West Point Series,"* while the careers of Darrin and Dalzell are set forth in the *"Annapolis Series,"* just as the adventures of Reade and Hazelton are set forth in the *"Young Engineers Series."*

At Annapolis, Darrin and Dalzell went through stirring times, indeed, as young midshipmen. Now, we again come upon them when they have become commissioned officers in the Navy. They are now seen at the outset of their careers as ensigns, ordered to duty aboard the dreadnought *"Long Island"* in the latter part of March, 1914.

Certainly the times were favorable for them to see much of active naval service, though as yet they could hardly more than guess the fact.

General Huerta, who had usurped the presidency of Mexico following the death——as suspected, by assassination——of the former president Madero—— had not been recognized as president by the United States. Some of Madero's friends and former followers, styling themselves the "Constitutionalists" had taken to the field in rebellion against the proclaimed authority of the dictator, Huerta. The two factions had long fought fiercely, and between the two warring parties that had rapidly reduced life in Mexico, to a state of anarchy, scores of Americans had been executed through spite, as it was alleged, and American women and children had also suffered at the hands of both factions.

Lives and property of citizens of European governments had been sacrificed, and now these European governments looked askance at the Washington government, which was expected to safeguard the rights of foreigners in Mexico.

To the disappointment and even the resentment of a large part of the people of the United States, the Washington government had moved slowly, expressing its hope that right would triumph in Mexico without outside armed interference.

This policy of the national administration had become known as watchful waiting. Many approved of it; other Americans demanded a policy of active intervention in Mexico to end the uncertainty and the misery caused by the helpless of many nations, who were ground between the opposing factions of revolution in Mexico.

With this brief explanation we will once more turn to the fortunes of Ensigns Dave and Dan.

At 6.45 the next morning the telephone bell began to tinkle in Dave's room. It continued to ring until Darrin rose, took down the receiver, and expressed, to the clerk, on duty below, his thanks for having been called.

"Turn out, Danny Grin!" Darry shouted from the bathroom. "Come, now, sir! Show a foot! Show a foot, sir!"

Drowsily, Dalzell thrust one bare foot out from under the sheet.

"Are you awake in sea-going order, sir?" Dave asked, jovially.

"Aye, aye, sir."

"Then remain awake, Mr. Dalzell, until I have been through the motions of a cold bath."

With that Darrin shut the door. From the bathroom came the sounds of a shower, followed by much splashing.

"Turn out the port watch, Mr. Dalzell," came, presently, through the closed bathroom door. "The bathroom watch is yours. Hose down, sir."

With that Dave stepped into his own room to dress. It was not long before the two young naval officers left their rooms, each carrying a suit case. To the top of each case was strapped a sword, emblem of officer's rank, and encased in chamois-skin.

Going below, the pair breakfasted, glancing, in the meantime, over morning newspapers.

Just before nine-thirty that same morning, our young naval officers, bent on joining their ship, stepped along briskly through the Brooklyn Navy Yard.

It was really an inspiring place. Sailors, marines and officers, too, were in evidence.

In the machine shops and about the docks thousands of men were performing what once would have passed for the work of giants. Huge pieces of steel were being shaped; heavy drays carried these pieces of steel; monster cranes hoisted them aboard ships lying at the docks or standing shored up in the dry docks. There was noise in the air; the spirit of work and accomplishment pervaded the place, for word had come from Washington that many ships might soon be needed in Mexican waters.

Eight dreadnoughts lay at their berths. Even as the boys crossed the great yard a cruiser was being warped in, after an eighteen-thousand mile voyage.

Alongside floating stages in the basins lay submarines and torpedo boat destroyers. A naval collier was being coaled. A Navy launch was in sight and coming closer, bearing a draft of marines bound for duty on one of the battleships.

Every sight spoke proudly of the naval might of a great nation, yet that might was not at all in proportion with the naval needs of such a vast country.

"It does an American good, just to be in a place like this, doesn't it?" asked Danny Grin.

"It does, indeed," Dave answered. Then, his bewilderment increasing, he turned to a marine who stood at a distance of some sixty feet from where he had halted.

"My man!" Dave called.

Instantly the marine wheeled about. Noting the suit cases, with the swords strapped to them, the marine recognized these young men in civilian attire as naval officers. Promptly his hand sought his cap visor in clean-cut salute, which both young ensigns as promptly returned.

"Be good enough to direct me to the `Long Island,'" Darrin requested.

"Yes, sir," and the marine, stepping closer, led the way past three large buildings.

"There she is, over there, sir," said the marine, a minute later, pointing. "Shall I carry your suit cases, sir, to the deck?"

"It won't be necessary, thank you," Darrin replied.

"Very good, sir," and again the marine saluted. Returning the salute, the two young officers hurried forward. As they strode along, their eyes feasting on the strong, proud lines of the dreadnought on which they were to serve, their staunch young hearts swelled with pride. And there, over the battleship's stern, floated the Flag, which they had taken most solemn oath to defend with their lives and with their honor, whether at home, or on the other side of the world.

In both breasts stirred the same emotions of love of country. Just then neither felt like speaking. They hastened on in silence. Up the gang-plank they strode. At a word from the officer on deck, two young sailors, serving as messengers, darted down the plank, saluting, then relieving the young officers of their suit cases.

Up the gang-plank, and aboard, walked the young ensigns. First the eyes of Ensigns Darrin and Dalzell sought the Flag. Bringing their heels together, standing erect, they faced the Stars and Stripes, flying at the stern, bringing their hands up smartly in salute. The officer of the deck returned to the youngsters the salute on behalf of the Flag.

Then Darrin and Dalzell approached the officer of the deck.

"I am Ensign Darrin, and I report having come aboard, sir," said Dave. Dan reported his own arrival in similar terms.

"My name is Trent," replied the officer of the deck, as he extended his right hand to each, in turn. "I hope you will like all of us; I know we shall like you."

Then to the messengers Lieutenant Trent gave the order to carry the suit cases to the rooms assigned to the two new ensigns. Dave and Dan followed the messengers through a corridor that led past the ward-room. The messengers halted before the curtained doorways of adjoining rooms, bags in left hands, their right hands up in salute.

"This is your room, sir," announced the messenger, in the precise tones of the service, while Dan's messenger indicated the other room.

"Some kind fate must have given us adjoining rooms," laughed Dave, when he realized that the two doors stood side by side.

As Darrin passed into his new quarters his first glance rested lovingly on the breech of a huge gun that pierced the armored side of the dreadnought.

"That's great!" thought the young ensign, jubilantly. "I shall have an emblem and a constant reminder of my duty to the United States!"

His second glance took in the polished top of a desk, over which hung an electric light.

There is no door to an officer's room; instead, a curtain hangs in place, screening the room from outside view. At one side, in the cabin, was another curtain, this screening the alcove in which lay the berth.

But Darrin did not stop to study his new quarters just then. There was a duty first to be performed. Opening his suit case, he took out the trousers and blouse of the blue undress uniform. Into this he changed as rapidly as he could, after which he brushed his hair before the little mirror, then put on his cap.

Next he fastened on his sword belt, after which he hung his sword at his side. An anxious head-to-foot glance followed, and Ensign Darrin found himself spick and span.

Now he stepped to Dan's door, calling in:

"May I come in, old fellow?"

"I'll be in a strange state of mind if you don't," Danny Grin answered.

Ensign Dalzell was putting the finishing touches to his own rapid toilet.

"I'm going to help myself to your card case," announced Dave, who already held a card of his own. Adding Dan's to that, Ensign Darrin stepped to the doorway, glancing quickly about him.

"Sentry!" Dave called.

"Sir!" answered a marine, stepping forward and giving the customary salute.

"Pass the word for a messenger, sentry!"

"Aye, aye, sir."

In a twinkling the messenger arrived, saluting.

"Take these cards to the captain, with the respectful compliments of Ensigns Darrin and Dalzell, and state that they await his permission to report to him."

"Aye, aye, sir."

In less than a minute the messenger returned, stating that the captain would receive them at once.

Captain Gales, a heavily-built, stately-looking man of fifty, rose from his desk in his office as the two young ensigns stepped through the door. The young men saluted their commander, then stood rigidly at attention.

"Mr. Darrin?" asked the captain, extending his hand, which Dave promptly clasped. Then Dan was greeted.

"Glad to have you with us," was all the captain said. Then, to the marine orderly who stood just within the door: "Show these gentlemen to the executive officer."

"He didn't ask after our folks, nor even if we liked the looks of the ship," Dalzell complained, in a whisper, as they followed the orderly.

"Be silent, Danny Grin!" urged Darrin, rebukingly. "This is no time for jesting."

Commander Bainbridge, the executive officer, received the young officers in his quarters. He proved to be more communicative, talking pleasantly with them for fully a minute and a half after the young men had introduced themselves, and had turned over to him the official papers connecting them with this dreadnought's personnel.

"Let me see, Mr. Dalzell," said Lieutenant Commander Bainbridge, referring to a record book on his desk, "you will be in Lieutenant Trent's division. Find Mr. Trent on the quarter deck and report to him. Mr. Darrin, you are assigned to Lieutenant Cantor's division. I will have an orderly show you to Mr. Cantor."

Dan departed first, walking very erect and feeling unusually elated, for Dalzell had thoroughly liked the appearance of Trent in their brief meeting, and believed that he would be wholly contented in serving under that superior.

While Dave's quarters were on the port side of the ship, Cantor's proved to be on the right side.

The messenger halted before a curtained doorway, rapping.

"Who's there?" called a voice inside.

"Messenger, sir, showing Ensign Darrin to Lieutenant Cantor, sir."

"Then you may go, messenger. Darrin, wait just an instant won't you, until I finish my toilet."

"Very good, sir."

A moment later the hail came from within.

"Right inside, Darrin!"

Dave entered, to find a somewhat older officer standing with extended hand. But Ensign Darrin could not believe his eyes when he found himself faced by the man who had annoyed the young woman on the night before——and that annoyer standing there erect and handsome in the uniform of a Navy lieutenant!

CHAPTER II

Their hands met, but in light clasp, without pretense of warmth.

Then Darrin fell back, bringing his right hand mechanically to a salute as he mumbled:

"I am Ensign Darrin, sir, and have been ordered, by the executive officer, to report to you for duty in your division."

"Very good, Mr. Darrin," rejoined the lieutenant. "My division goes on watch at eight bells noon. You will report to me on the quarter deck at that time."

"Very good, sir."

With a quick step Lieutenant Cantor reached the curtain, holding it slightly aside and peering out into the passage-way. His face was red, but there was one portion that was redder still.

"I see," Dave reflected, "that Cantor still wears the welt that I printed on his cheek last night. But it staggers me," he thought, gravely, "to find such a fellow holding an officer's commission in the Navy."

Satisfied that there were no eavesdroppers near, Lieutenant Cantor stepped back, facing the young ensign, whom he looked over with an expression of mingled hate and distress.

"I believe we have met before," said Cantor, with a quick, hissing indrawing of his breath.

"To my very great regret, we have, sir," Darrin answered, coldly.

"Last night!"

"Yes, sir."

"And you behaved abominably, Darrin!"

"Indeed, sir?"

"You interfered," Lieutenant Cantor continued, "with one of the most important affairs of my life."

"Yes, sir? With one of the most shameful, I should imagine, sir."

Ensign Darrin's tone was officially respectful, but his glance cold. He felt no respect for Cantor, and could see no reason why he should pretend respect.

"I had a strong belief that I should see you again," Cantor continued, his gleaming eyes turned on the new ensign.

"You knew me to be of the Navy, sir?"

"I did not, Darrin, nor did you know me to be of the Navy. Otherwise, it is not likely that you would have behaved as you did."

"If I had known you to be the fleet admiral, Mr. Cantor, my conduct could not have been different, under the circumstances."

"Darrin, you are a fool!" hissed the division officer.

"I am much obliged to you, sir, for your good opinion," Dave answered, in an even voice.

For an instant the lieutenant frowned deeply. Then his face cleared.
His glance became almost friendly as he continued:

"Darrin, I think it probable that you will have a chance to repair your bad work of last night."

"Sir?"

"Last night you told me that you had noted the number of the taxicab in which the young woman escaped me."

"I did, sir."

"Perhaps you still remember that number. Indeed, I am sure that you must."

"I do remember the number, sir."

"What was it?" asked Cantor, eagerly.

"That number, sir, so far as I am concerned," Ensign Darrin answered, tranquilly, "is a woman's secret."

"It is a secret which I have a right to know," Lieutenant Cantor went on pressingly.

"The number, sir, I would not dream of giving you without the permission of the young woman herself," Darrin answered, slowly. "As I do not even know her name, it is unlikely that I shall be able to secure that permission."

"Darrin, it is my right to receive an answer to my question," insisted Cantor, his eyes glittering coldly.

"You will have to find out from some one other than myself, then," was Dave's calm answer.

"Darrin, you force me to tell you more than I really ought to tell. I am going to marry that young woman!"

"Is the young woman aware of your intentions, sir?" Dave demanded, quietly.

"Yes! Darrin, I tell you, I am going to marry that young woman, and it is most imperative that I should see her as early as possible. Give me the number of that taxicab, and I can find the driver and learn where he took her. Now, what are you smiling at, Darrin?"

"It struck me, sir, that you should already know the address of a young woman whom you are engaged to marry."

Lieutenant Cantor repressed an exclamation of impatience and bit his lips.

"Of course I know her home address," he deigned to reply, "but she is not a New Yorker. Her home is at a considerable distance, and I do not know where to find her in New York. Give me that taxicab number and I shall be able to secure shore leave. By this evening I shall have found her."

"You do not expect me to wish you luck in a matter like this, sir?" Ensign Darrin inquired.

"I expect you to give me the number of that taxicab, and at once," replied Cantor. He did not raise his voice, but there was compelling fury in his tone.

"I have already declined to do that, sir," Dave insisted.

"Darrin, do you realize that I am your superior?" demanded the lieutenant.

"I am aware, sir, that you are my superior officer," Darrin answered, with strong emphasis on the word "officer."

"And you refuse to please me in a trifling matter?"

"Pardon me, sir, but from the little that I saw and heard, I cannot believe that your discovery of her address would be regarded by the young woman as a trifling matter."

"Do you persist in refusing to tell me that taxicab number?" hissed Lieutenant Cantor.

"Sir, as a gentleman, I must," Dave rejoined. For a full half minute Lieutenant Cantor stared at his subordinate in speechless anger. Then, when he could command his voice somewhat, he resumed:

"Oh, very good, you—-you young—-puppy!"

Another brief interval of silence, and the lieutenant continued, in a crisp, official tone:

"Mr. Darrin, go to the division bulletin board and get an accurate copy of the roster of the division. Also make a copy of our station bills. You will then report to me on the quarter deck just before eight bells, noon."

"Aye, aye, sir! Any further orders?"

"None!"

Cantor stood there, an appealing look in his eyes, but Dave, saluting, turned on his heel and went out.

"So that is the fellow who is to teach me the duties and the ideals of the service," Dave Darrin reflected, disgustedly, as he stepped briskly around to port. "A magnificent prospect ahead of me, if I must depend upon the instructions and the official favor of a bully and a scoundrel like Cantor! And he can make it hot for me, too, if he has a mind to do so! Don't I know how easy that ought to be for him? I shall have, indeed, a lot of pleasure in my service on this ship, with Cantor for my division officer!"

Mindful of orders, Darrin's first act was to copy the division roster and the station bills. These he took to his room, placing them in a drawer of the desk, for future study. For the present, he wanted to get out into the open air.

Though Ensign Dalzell had been directed to report on the quarter deck, he was not now there. Dave walked about by himself until Lieutenant Trent came over and spoke to him.

"Dalzell is busy, I suppose, sir?" Dave inquired.

"Forward and below, directing the stowage of stores," replied Trent. "Have you been detailed to a division yet, Mr. Darrin?"

"Yes, sir; to Lieutenant Cantor's division."

"Ah, so?" inquired Trent. He did not say more, from which Dave wondered if Trent did not like Cantor. If such were the case, then Darrin's opinion of Lieutenant Trent would run all the higher.

"Cantor is a very efficient officer," Trent said, after a pause, not long enough to be construed unfavorably.

Dave did not answer this, for he could think of nothing to say.

"Some of our newest youngsters haven't wholly liked him," Trout went on, with a smile. "I fancy that perhaps he works them a bit too grillingly."

"After four years at the Naval Academy," smiled Ensign Darrin, "it puzzles me to understand how any officer can resent grilling."

"You'll find life very different on one of these big ships," Lieutenant Trout continued. "You will soon begin to realize that we are in a cramped atmosphere. With fifteen hundred officers and men abroad there is barely elbow room at any time, and sometimes not that."

"This ship looks big enough to carry a small city full of people," Darrin smiled.

"See here!" Trent stepped to the starboard rail, looking forward.

"Just look ahead, and see the magnificent distance to the bow," continued the officer of the deck. "We call a ship 'she,' Darrin, and let me assure you, 'she' is some girl! Look at the magnificent length and breadth. Yet, when we are at sea, you will soon begin to realize how cramped the life is."

After chatting a little longer with Lieutenant Trent, Ensign Darrin started forward along the decks, taking in all he could see of this huge, floating castle.

Presently he returned to the quarter-deck, but Lieutenant Trent was busy with a lieutenant of the marine guard. Dave stepped inside. Almost immediately he heard a step at his side. Glancing around, Dave looked into the face of Lieutenant Cantor.

"A while ago I noticed you talking with Trent," Dave's division officer remarked, in a low voice.

"Yes, sir."

"Did you discuss me?"

"Yes, sir."

"What did you say, Darrin?"

"I mentioned that you were my division officer."

"Did Trent say anything?"

"Mr. Trent said that you were a very efficient officer."

"Did you tell him anything—-about—-er—-about last night?"

"Nothing," Dave answered.

"Positive about that?" insinuated Cantor.

"Sir," Dave answered, "I am an officer and, I trust—-a gentleman."

"Then you told Trent nothing about last night?"

"I have already told you, sir, that I didn't."

"Nor to anyone else on this ship?" pressed the lieutenant.

"I told Dalzell, last night, that I had met with a stranger who was———"

"That will do!" snapped Cantor.

"Very good, sir."

"Have you told Dalzell about me since coming aboard?"

"I have not."

"And you won't?" pressed Cantor.

"On that point, sir, I decline to pledge myself," Darrin responded, with unusual stiffness.

"Darrin, do you want to make an enemy?"

"Mr. Cantor, I never, at any time, wish to make an enemy. I am not trying to make one of you."

"I will regard that as a promise from you," returned Cantor, then moved quickly away.

"It would have been better," murmured Darrin, softly, turning and regarding the moving figure, "if you had heard me out. However, Mr. Cantor, though you are not now here to hear me say it, I did not promise silence. Yet it is difficult to conceive what would make me open my mouth on the subject of last night's happening. I have never been a tale-bearer, and, much as I may despise that fellow, and the affront that he offers the Navy, in remaining in the service, I fancy his secret is safe from all——except Dalzell. Danny and I haven't yet begun to have secrets from each other."

Presently Dan Dalzell, wearing his sword and pulling on his white gloves as he came, appeared, walking aft. There was time only for a smiling nod, for Dave suddenly remembered, with a start that it was time for him to report for change of watch.

Hastening down the passage-way Dave hung his sword on, then hastily rummaged the suit case for a pair of white gloves that he had previously tucked in there.

Hastening, he reached the deck just as the watch was being changed. With quick step Ensign Darrin took his momentary post. Then, when the old watch had gone off duty, Lieutenant Cantor turned to his subordinate with a frown.

"Ensign Darrin, you made a bad beginning, sir," declared the new watch officer, crisply. "In the future, I trust you will be more mindful of the responsibility of an officer in setting his men an example in punctuality. If this occurs again, sir, I shall feel it my duty to turn in report of your negligence!"

Several men of the watch and two of the marine guard hoard this rebuke administered. Dave Darrin's face flushed, then paled from the humiliation of the rebuke. Yet he had been guilty of an actual breach of discipline, minor though it was, and could not dispute Cantor's right to reprove him.

"I very much regret my negligence, sir," Dave answered, saluting, but he bit his lip in the same instant for he realized how thoroughly his superior officer enjoyed the privilege of administering the rebuke.

From inside Dan Dalzell heard the words.

At once, on the stroke of eight bells, the mess signal was hung to the breeze. While that flag flew no one was admitted to the battleship unless he belonged on board.

Then appeared a little Filipino mess servant, who asked Dave and Dan to follow him to their assigned seats.

"Am I permitted to go to mess, sir?" Dave asked of Lieutenant Cantor.

"Yes," was the short answer.

While the signal flew the sergeant of the marine guard was in charge at the quarter-deck gang plank. There was no need of a commissioned officer there.

To their delight Darrin and Dalzell found themselves assigned to seats at the table together.

Lieutenant Trent stepped down, introducing the new arrivals to the officers beside whom, and opposite whom they sat.

"I was sorry to hear you get that calling down," Dalzell whispered to his chum, as soon as that was possible under the cover of the conversation of others. "Why did Lieutenant Cantor seem to enjoy his privilege so much?"

After a covert glance, to make sure that he was not in danger of being overheard, Darrin replied, in an undertone:

"Lieutenant Cantor was the man of whom I told you last night."

"Not the——"

"Yes," Dave nodded.

"But it seems incredible that an officer of our Navy could be guilty of any such conduct," Dalzell gasped, his eyes large with amazement. "Are you sure?"

"Didn't you notice the welt on Mr. Cantor's cheek?" Dave asked, dryly.

Danny Grin nodded, then fell silent over his plate.

After the meal Lieutenant Trent saw to it that both the new ensigns were introduced to such officers as they had not met already.

"We can't possibly remember all their names——scores of 'em!" gasped Dan, as the two young officers stood outside the mess.

"We'll learn every name and face before very long," Darrin answered. "But I mustn't stand talking," Dave went on, as he again hung his sword at his side. "I'm on duty, and can't stand another call-down."

"Are you going to tell what Cantor did last night?" Dan queried.

"No; and don't you tell, either!"

"Small fear of my babbling *your* business, David, little Giant!" assured Dalzell. "You are strong enough to go in and slay your own Goliath."

Drawing on his white gloves, Dave Darrin stepped alertly to the quarter deck, to find himself facing the frown of Lieutenant Cantor.

CHAPTER III

THE JUNIOR WORM TURNS

"Wonder what my man has in store for me?" flashed through Dave's mind, as he saluted his division commander.

But Cantor, after returning the salute, merely turned away to pace the deck.

Presently, however, the lieutenant stepped over to Darrin, when the pair had the quarterdeck to themselves.

"Are you going to tell me?" murmured the lieutenant, his burning gaze on the frank young face before him.

"Tell you what, sir?" Dave asked.

"That taxicab number?"

"No, sir!"

"Think!"

"When I have decided that a given course of conduct is the only course possible to a gentleman," Ensign Darrin replied, "I have no further occasion to give thought to that subject."

"Darrin, you might make me your friend!" urged his superior officer.

"That would be delightful, sir."

"Darrin, don't try to be ironical with me!"

Dave remained silent.

"If you don't care for me for your friend, Darrin," Cantor warned him, "it is possible, on the other hand, to make an enemy of me. As an enemy you would not find me wanting either in resource or opportunity."

"Have you any orders for me, sir?" asked Darrin, coolly. That was as near as he could come, courteously, to informing Cantor that he wished from him none but official communications.

"Pardon me, sir," said Cantor, and stepped away to salute Commander Bainbridge, who had just appeared on the quarter-deck. There was a low-toned conversation between the two officers. Then, as the pair exchanged salutes, and Bainbridge went on to the captain's quarters, Lieutenant Cantor came back to his selected victim.

"Darrin, you will go below and finish the watch, loading stores in the number four hold. I will pass the word for the petty officer who will have charge under you, and he will show you to the hold. If you wish you may put on dungarees, for it is rough work down there."

"My baggage has not come aboard, sir," Dave replied. "This is the only uniform I have."

In his perturbed state of mind, it did not occur to the young ensign that he could draw dungarees—-the brown overall suit that is worn by officers and crew alike when doing rough work about the ship, from the stores, nor did Cantor appear to notice his reply.

The messenger came, and brought Riley, the coxswain of one of the gigs.

"Coxswain, Ensign Darrin will take charge of the shipping of the stores in number four hold," Cantor announced. "Show him the way to the hold and receive his instructions."

Dave was speedily engaged between decks, in charge of tire work of some twenty men of the crew. At the hatch above, a boatswain's mate had charge of the lowering of the stores.

"It would be a pity to spoil your uniform, sir," declared Coxswain Riley. "If you'll allow me, sir, I'll spare you all of the dirtiest work."

"To shirk my duty would be a bad beginning of my service on this ship," smiled Darrin. "Thank you, Coxswain, but I'll take my share of the rough work."

The hold was close and stifling. Although a cool breeze was blowing on deck, there was little air in number two hold. In ten minutes Darrin found himself bathed in perspiration. Dust from barrels and packing cases hung heavy in that confined space. The grime settled on his perspiring face and stuck there.

"Look out, sir, or you'll get covered with pitch from some of these barrels," Riley warned Dave, respectfully.

"One uniform spoiled is nothing," Dave answered with a smile. "Do not be concerned about me."

Officer and men were suffering alike in that close atmosphere. By the time the watch was ended Dave Darrin was truly a pitchy, soiled, perspiration-soaked sight.

Danny Grin, who reported to relieve his chum, looked rough and ready enough in a suit of dungarees that he had drawn.

"I should have had brains enough to remember that I, too, could have drawn dungarees," Dave grunted, as he and his chum exchanged salutes. Then the relieved young officer hastened above to report the completion of his duty to his division commander, who would be furious if kept waiting.

Dave glanced toward Cantor's quarters, then realized that the lieutenant must still be on the quarter deck.

In his haste to be punctual, Darrin forgot his sword and white gloves, which he had left in his own cabin on the way to duty between decks. Without these appurtenances of duty on the quarter-deck, Darrin made haste aft, found his division commander, saluted and reported his relief.

"Mr. Darrin," boomed Cantor, in a tone of high displeasure, "don't you know that an officer reporting to the quarter-deck when in any but dungaree clothes, should wear his gloves and sword. Go and get them, sir—-and don't keep me waiting beyond my watch time when I have shore leave!"

Again red-faced and humiliated, Ensign Darrin saluted, wheeled, made haste to his quarters, then returned wearing sword and gloves. This time he saluted and made his report in proper form.

"Mr. Darrin," said his division officer, scathingly, "this is the second time to-day that I have had to teach you the things you should have learned in your first week at Annapolis. You are making a bad beginning, sir."

Dave saluted, but this time did not answer in words.

"You may go, Mr. Darrin, and hereafter I trust to find in you a more attentive and clear-headed officer."

Lieutenant Cantor did not hold his tone low. It is the privilege of an officer to rebuke an enlisted man publicly, and as severely as the offense warrants, and it is the further privilege of an officer to make his rebuke to a subordinate commissioned officer as sharp and stinging as he chooses.

Saluting, without a word, Darrin wheeled and walked to his quarters.

"Cantor will certainly have abundant opportunity to make things warm for me," reflected Darrin, as he sat down before the desk in his cabin. "I wonder what I am to do, in order to keep my self-respect and keep my hands off the fellow. It would probably end my career in the Navy if I struck him on this ship."

For some minutes Darrin sat in a rather dejected frame of mind, reviewing his first acquaintance with this official cur, and the things that had happened on shipboard since.

"I suppose I could ask for a different detail," Dave mused, forlornly. "Undoubtedly, though, I wouldn't get the detail, unless I gave what were

24

considered sufficiently good reasons, and I can't tell tales on my division commander, cur though I know him to be."

In the passage outside, sounded passing footsteps and a laugh. Dave felt his face flush, for he recognized the voice of Lieutenant Cantor.

"Danny Grin is a good chum," reflected Darrin, "but in this affair he can't advise me any better than I can advise myself. I wish I could talk freely with some older officer, who knows shipboard life better. But if I were to go to any older officer with such a tale as I have, it would———"

"In, Mr. Darrin?" sounded a cheery voice, and Commander Bainbridge, the executive officer, stood in the doorway, bringing young Darrin to his feet in prompt salute.

"I was passing, Darrin, and so I called," announced the executive officer. "Otherwise, I would have summoned you to my office. Lieutenant Cantor has secured shore leave until eleven o'clock to-night. As we are busy aboard, Mr. Cantor's division is due for watch duty at eight bells this evening. As Mr. Cantor has shore leave you will report as officer of the deck until relieved by Lieutenant Cantor on his return to the ship. At any time between now and four bells report at my office and sign for these instructions."

"Aye, aye, sir."

Returning the ensign's salute, the executive officer next regarded Darrin's untidy appearance with some displeasure.

"Mr. Darrin," Commander Bainbridge continued, "I note that you must have been on hard duty. No officer, after being relieved, is entitled to retain an untidy appearance longer than is necessary. You should have bathed, sir, and attired yourself becomingly. Neatness is the first requisite in the service."

"I shall be glad to do that sir," Dave answered, respectfully, "as soon as my baggage comes aboard. At present this is the only uniform I have."

"That alters the case, Mr. Darrin," replied the executive officer, kindly. "In case, however, your baggage does not arrive between now and dinner-time, you will not be warranted in going to the ward-room, unless you can borrow a uniform that fits you as well as one of your own."

"I shall be very careful on that point, sir," Dave answered, respectfully, with another salute, returning which Commander Bainbridge departed.

Ten minutes later Darrin's baggage was delivered. In their proper places the young ensign hung his various uniforms, placed his shoes according to regulation, and stowed his linen and underclothing in the wardrobe drawers.

After this a most welcome bath followed. Dave then dressed with care in a fresh blue uniform, stepped to the executive officer's office and signed for his evening orders.

There was time for fifteen minutes in the open air, after which Dave returned to his quarters to dress for dinner. This done, he stepped outside, knowing that the summons to the wardroom would soon come.

At first Dave was the only officer at that point. Commander Bainbridge soon joined him.

A desperate thought entering his mind, Dave addressed the commander as soon as his salute had been returned.

"Sir, may I ask you a question connected with my own personal affairs?" he asked.

"Certainly," replied the executive officer.

"I was wondering, sir, if it would be wise for me to seek counsel from an older officer if at any time I found myself threatened with trouble, or, at least, with unpleasantness."

"It would be a very wise course on your part, Darrin," replied Commander Bainbridge, though he regarded the ensign's face with keen scrutiny. "An older officer should always esteem it a pleasure, as well as a duty, to advise a younger officer. I take an interest in all the officers of this ship. If there is anything in which I can advise you, you may command me."

"Thank you, sir. But, if you will permit me to frame an instance, if the advice that I asked of you might tend to prejudice you against one of your subordinate officers, would it be wiser for me to seek counsel of some officer not higher in rank than the officer whom I have just supposed?"

"That is to say, Mr. Darrin, that the advice you might otherwise wish to ask of me might be taken in the light of a complaint against an officer who is one of my subordinates, and against whom you would not wish to carry tales? In that case, you would, by all means, show good judgment consulting a younger officer. But remember, Darrin, that not all men are equally wise. Be very careful whom you select at any time as adviser. And remember that, for any advice that you may properly ask of me, you may come to me without hesitation."

"Thank you, sir. I trust you realize how deeply grateful I am to you," Dave protested earnestly.

As other officers came up, Commander Bainbridge cut the discussion short by turning to greet the arrivals.

Dinner in the ward-room was the formal meal of the day. The table, covered with snowy damask, glittered with crystal and silver. Silent, soft-moving little Filipinos, in their white mess suits, glided about, serving noiselessly.

At the head of the table sat Commander Bainbridge, the executive officer, for the captain of a battleship dines in solitary state in his own apartments. On either side of the executive officer sat the other officers, in two long rows, according to their rank. On either side of the Commander were seated the officers with rank of lieutenant commander. Next to them were the lieutenants, senior grade. After them came the lieutenants, junior grade. At the foot of the table was a group of ensigns, the lowest in rank of commissioned officers of the Navy.

Course followed course, and good humor prevailed at the officers' table. Now and then a good joke or a witty sally called forth hearty laughter. Here and there officers, dismissing laughter for the time being, talked of graver matters.

Danny Grin soon found time to murmur the question:

"How did you get along with your tyrant this afternoon?"

"No better," Dave answered, moodily.

"Did he rake you over the coals again?"

"Yes." Then Darrin detailed the circumstances.

"I am afraid he has it in for you, all right," muttered Danny Grin, scowling.

"He'll report me as often as he can, I don't doubt," Dave replied. "If he can bring me up before a general court-martial, all the better."

"I'm sorry you're not in Trent's division," Dan sighed. "He's a gentleman——a regular, sea-going officer."

"Sea-going" is the highest praise that can be given in Navy circles.

"If I were in Trent's division, probably you'd have fallen under Cantor," Darrin suggested.

"That would have been all right," nodded Dalzell, cheerily. "Cantor has no direct cause to hate me, as he has in your case. Besides, I'd do a good many things to a mean superior that you wouldn't. If I had to stand watch with Cantor, and he tried any queer treatment of me, I'd find a way to make his life miserable. I believe I've shown some skill in that line in the past."

"You surely have," Darrin nodded. "But I don't like to spring traps for my superior officers to fall into."

"Not even in self-defence?" challenged Dalzell.

"Not even to save myself," Darrin declared. At eight bells, in Lieutenant Cantor's absence, Darrin took the watch trick alone as officer of the deck until six bells, or eleven o'clock that night.

There was not much to do. Now and then a shore leave man, sailor or marine, reported coming on board. Darrin made a note of the man's return and entered the time. Twice, a messenger brought some small order from the executive officer. Yet it was a dull watch, with the ship docked and nothing of importance happening.

"Cantor will soon be back," thought Dave, at last, slipping out his watch and glancing at it under the light that came from the cabin. His timepiece showed the time to be five minutes to eleven.

But a quarter of an hour passed, and no Lieutenant Cantor appeared. More time slipped by without the lieutenant's return.

"That doesn't sound much like the punctuality that is required of a naval officer," Dave told himself, in some disquiet.

Then finally a step was heard on the gangplank. Lieutenant Cantor came briskly up over the side, halting on the deck and saluting toward the stern, where the colors flew until sundown.

"Mr. Darrin, I've come on board," reported the lieutenant, turning in time to catch Dave's salute.

He stepped closer, to add:

"You will enter a note that I came on board at 10.58."

"The time is eleven-forty, sir," Dave reminded his superior, at the same time displaying his watch.

"Note that I came on board at 10.58," insisted Cantor, frowning.

"Sentry!" called Dave, briskly.

"Aye, aye, sir!"

"Note the time on the chronometer inside," Darrin ordered.

"Aye, aye, sir." Then, returning the marine sentry answered:

"It's eleven-forty, sir."

Dave made the entry of the lieutenant's return.

"You infernal trouble-maker," hissed Cantor, as the sentry paced on. "You dragged that sentry into it, just so you would have supporting testimony of the time I came aboard! I'll pay you back for that! Look out for trouble, Mr.

Darrin!"

CHAPTER IV

THE WARD-ROOM HEARS REAL NEWS

Hurrying to the now empty office of the executive officer, Cantor made correct entry of his return to ship on the record, then hurried to his own quarters, and with almost the speed of magic, slipped into his undress uniform, belted on his sword, and appeared smartly on the quarter-deck.

For two minutes he paid no heed to Darrin, save to return the salute with which the young ensign greeted his superior's return to command of the deck.

Presently, however, Lieutenant Cantor stepped over to say in an undertone:

"Darrin, you have made the wrong start, and I see that you are bound to keep it up."

"I am trying to do my duty, sir," Darrin returned. "I could not consent to make a false official return."

"Officers often have to do that for each other," Cantor went on, in the same low tone, "and they do it willingly as between comrades."

It was on the tip of Darrin tongue to retort that he didn't believe any true officer, being a man of honor, could stoop to making a false official report. Yet he instantly thought better of it, and forced back the sarcastic retort that rose to his lips.

"You're not going to succeed in the Navy, sir," Cantor continued, then, seeing the young ensign's face still impassive, he added, with a malicious leer:

"Since you are determined to make an enemy of me, Darrin, I shall do my best to see to it that you have short shrift in the service."

"Of that I haven't a doubt," Dave returned, but he caught himself in time and said it under his breath.

Then came the changing of the watch. Trent and Dalzell appeared and went on duty.

Formally, Dave wished his division commander good night, Cantor answering only with a grunt.

Returning to his stateroom, Dave threw off belt and sword, hung up his cap, then sat down in his desk chair, leaning back and steadily regarding the breech of the great gun.

"I wonder if any other young officer in the service is at the mercy of such a brute," Darrin asked himself, wretchedly. "I love good discipline, but there's one thing wrong with the service, and that is, the ease with which a dishonorable officer can render the life of his subordinate miserable. It ought not to be possible, and yet I don't see any way of preventing it. I wish I could talk with a gentleman like Lieutenant Trent, but he would only regard me as a tale-bearer, and after that he would have no use for me. One thing I can see clearly. Cantor is likely to have me broken and kicked out of the service if I am forced to remain in his division week after week."

Then, realizing that his time was slipping away, Darrin hastily undressed and got into his berth. It was a long time, though, before sleep came to him.

In the morning Lieutenant Cantor was obliged to listen meekly to a long discourse by the executive officer on the virtue of punctuality in a naval officer. The offender told of a car block in New York that had made it impossible for him to return on time.

"Lieutenant Cantor," returned the executive officer, dryly, "a careful officer will allow himself sufficient margin of time to make it morally certain that he can be back to his duty on time. Now, sir——-"

But at this moment an apprentice messenger, standing in the doorway, his right hand drawn up in salute, attracted the gaze of Commander Bainbridge:

"The captain" compliments, sir; will the executive officer report to him at once."

"That is all—-for the present—-Lieutenant Cantor," said Commander Bainbridge, rising from his chair and hastening out.

"And all this, on account of a puppy of a junior who will not use sense and reason at the request of a superior officer!" ground Cantor between his teeth. "I shall pay Darrin for this, and for that greater insult, too."

Some minutes before the call to breakfast was due, Darrin and Dalzell appeared from their quarters and walked aft to where a group of the "*Long Island's*" officers stood. Three or four of them had newspapers in their hands.

"It's time the government did something!" exclaimed one lieutenant commander, testily.

"We're going to do something, soon," asserted another officer, with a snap of his jaws.

"When?" demanded a third officer, while several men laughed derisively.

"We'll have to," continued the second speaker. "Every day the Mexican situation becomes worse. The usurper, Huerta, is becoming more of a menace all the time. He has no regard for the rights of any one, but himself. And he is unable to do more, in the field, than to accept defeat after defeat at the hands of the rebels under that former bandit chief, 'Pancho' Villa. Both the so-called Federals and the rebels, in Mexico, are doing their best to make Mexico a hotbed of incurable anarchy. Scores of American citizens have been murdered ruthlessly, and American women have been roughly treated. British subjects have been shot without the shadow of an excuse, and other foreigners have been maltreated. This country claims to uphold the Monroe Doctrine, which prevents European nations from interfering with force in affairs on this continent. If that is the case, then the United States must put an end to the numberless outrages against Americans and Europeans that take place every week in Mexico. That once orderly republic, Mexico, is now nothing better than a school for instruction in wholesale murder and in the ruthless riding over of the rights of all aliens residing or traveling in that country. These aliens have every right to protection."

"Quite true," remarked another officer. "But what has that to do with the United States? What has there been in our conduct during the past three or four years to indicate that we would take any strong-handed action to make life and property safe in Mexico?"

"We shall soon interfere," predicted the former speaker, confidently. "Affairs in Mexico are now nearing a crisis. The United States will no longer be called a civilized and honorable nation if Army and Navy men are not sent to Mexico to uphold our government and the rights of American citizens living there."

"Do you think, Holton, that will happen before you and I have been put on the retired list as white-haired rear admirals?" asked another officer, half-jeeringly.

"You will find," insisted Lieutenant Holton, "that we shall soon be listening to the thunder of our American naval guns at Vera Cruz, Tampico, or some other port on the shores of the Gulf of Mexico."

"Hurrah!" came from the throats of a dozen officers, but the cheer was not a very confident one. Too long had the United States been patient in the face of one insult or injury after another. General Huerta, in Mexico City, and Carranza and Villa, in the west and north of that country, had headed factions, neither of which seemed to care about Mexico's good name in the world at large. Maltreated Americans demanded punishment of the Mexican offenders, but the United States had been engaged in patiently waiting and watching, only once in a while sending a feeble protest either to the Federal or the Constitutionalist leaders in that murder-ridden country of Mexico.

Mess-call sounded to breakfast. The officers filed into their places at table; then, on observing that the executive officer was not in his place at the head of the table, they remained standing by their chairs.

A minute afterward Commander Bainbridge entered with brisk stride, going to his place and giving the seating signal as he said:

"Pardon my tardiness, gentlemen; the captain detained me on a most urgent matter."

After that the buzz of conversation broke loose. Breakfast orders were taken by the white-coated, noiseless Filipino servants. When all had been served, the executive officer glanced up, then rose.

"The attendants will withdraw," he ordered. "Orderly!"

"Aye, aye, sir!" responded the marine orderly on post just inside the door.

"As soon as the attendants have gone outside, orderly, you will chose the door from the outside, and remain there to keep any one from entering the room."

"Aye, aye, sir!" responded the orderly, who then followed the last attendant outside, closing the door after him.

"Gentlemen," continued the executive officer, remaining standing, "Captain Gales sent for me this morning, to make a most important communication. With his approval I am going to tell you something of what he said. In a word, then, this ship is ordered to be fitted for a cruise to Mexico in the shortest time possible. Within three or four days we must be on our way to Mexican waters.

"We are to go with bunkers filled with coal. We are to carry abundant clothing supplies for tropical service. We are to carry all the large and small arms ammunition that we can stow away. We are to take on food supplies to our fullest commissary capacity. In a word, we are to go prepared for any emergency.

"Now, gentlemen, on account of our departure at the earliest moment, every officer will be needed on board all the time. Unless for some extraordinary reason, shore leave will not be granted to any officer. The watch-word will be 'hustle.' Thank you, gentlemen, for your attention."

In an instant there was clamor in the wardroom. Twenty officers spoke at once, then subsided. Finally only the voice of Lieutenant Commander Denton was heard as he inquired:

"Sir, are we entitled to ask any questions?"

"I will answer any questions that I may properly," smiled the executive officer.

"We are going to Mexico, sir, in fighting trim, are we not?"

"I think what I have already said will indicate that," came Commander Bainbridge's reply.

"Has anything happened in Mexico," continued Denton, "which makes it imperative for us to fight there?"

"Nothing, so far as I know," answered the executive officer, "other than the usual daily outrages that are disgracing the fair name of Mexico."

"Then nothing of unusual importance has happened, which would make us sure that we are heading for Mexico on a definite fighting errand?"

"I have no knowledge that we are actually going to fight in Mexico," replied Commander Bainbridge. "It has occurred to me that this ship, and others of the line, are being ordered to Mexico as a hint to Federals and rebels alike that the United States possesses force enough to bring all Mexicans to their senses."

Having made this last reply, Commander Bainbridge touched a button. The ward-room door was thrown open, and the mess-servants once more entered.

But now a new note crept into the talk. The fact that the "*Long Island*" was to carry to Mexican waters full supplies of all kinds, including small and large ammunition, was enough to satisfy these officers of the Navy that the government at Washington had an important move on hand, and that move was expected to bring about armed conflict between the two countries.

"Now, am I a dreamer?" demanded Lieutenant Holton of those about him.

The two most excited officers present were also the newest on board the "*Long Island*." At the thought of active service against an enemy, Dave Darrin and Dan Dalzell fairly tingled.

"This is the greatest news we could possibly get," beamed Danny Grin, turning to his chum.

"It seems too great to be true," replied Ensign Darrin. "Danny, the Mexicans have been boasting that we don't *dare* tackle them and stir up that Mexican hornet's nest. If we get a chance, the American Navy will show them—-and the world—-something well worth remembering!"

Both Darrin and Dalzell had already been notified that they were detailed to "day duty" for that day. This meant that they would have no watch duty to stand, but would be employed through the day, while watch duty fell to the lot of others.

While Dalzell was to go below, with Trent, aiding in the storage of shells in the magazine, Darrin was ordered to report to Lieutenant Cantor to supervise the oiling of mechanisms of the guns of Cantor's division, and, later, to perform other important duties.

"Your face is flushed," sneered Cantor, when he found an opportunity to speak aside with Dave. "You are dreaming of active service in war, perhaps."

"Yes, sir," said Dave, simply.

"Look out that war service doesn't bring you disgrace, instead of honor or glory," warned Cantor, darkly.

"What do you mean, sir?"

"You have made me your enemy, and I am a good hater," retorted Lieutenant Cantor.

"You will be under my orders, and I may find a chance———"

Lieutenant Cantor finished only with an expressive shrug of his shoulders.

Though Dave Darrin felt a tremor of uneasiness, his eyes flashed back honest indignation and contempt for so unworthy a superior officer.

CHAPTER V

April, in the tropics!

Four miles off the coast of Mexico, east of the historic port of Vera Cruz, the United States dreadnought, "*Long Island*," moved along at slow cruising speed.

The few days out from New York had brought marked changes in climate. While people in New York found the weather still cold, here in Mexican waters, officers and men alike were in the white uniforms of the tropics—-all save those whose work below compelled them to wear dungarees.

On the bridge forward, two officers paced at a time. During the night hours there were always three there.

Aft, on the quarter-deck, marines were going through the rifle gymnastic drill. In some of the divisions officers and men were busy at the big gun drills. Others were cleaning a ship that always seemed spotless. The few that were off duty gathered wherever they could find room, for a battleship at sea, with her full complement of officers and men on board, is a crowded affair.

No other ship of the American fleet was in sight, but two operators, constantly on duty in the wireless room, kept the "*Long Island*" in constant touch with a score of vessels of the United States Navy.

"Have you any idea what we're doing here?" asked Danny Grin, as he and Dave met on the superstructure.

"No idea whatever," Ensign Darrin admitted. "I have noticed, though, that the officers on the bridge keep a constant lookout ashore. See; two of them, even now, have their binoculars trained on the shore."

"I don't see anything over there," replied Dalzell, "except a house or a small village here and there. I looked through the binoculars a little while ago, and to me it appeared a country that was about nine-tenths swamp."

"In the event of sending landing parties ashore," Dave hinted, "we might have to fight in one of those swamps. When it comes to fighting in the tangles and mazes of a swamp, I fancy the Mexicans have had a whole lot more experience than we have had."

"Why should we have to send landing parties so far from Vera Cruz?" Dan demanded, opening his eyes.

"We're only forty or fifty miles east of Vera Cruz," Darrin went on. "Danny boy, Vera Cruz is supposed to have a garrison, at present, of only about eight hundred of General Huerta's Mexican Federals. But suppose it was rumored that the Americans intended to land at Vera Cruz. Isn't it likely that the garrison would be greatly increased?"

"Let 'em increase their old garrison," smiled Dalzell, contemptuously. "The first landing parties from our fleet would drive out any kind of a Mexican garrison that Huerta could put in that town."

"Exactly," nodded Dave, "and then the Mexicans would naturally fall back."

"We can chase 'em," asserted Ensign Dalzell.

"Certainly, but a large force of Mexicans might fall back along the coast, through the swampy country we are now facing."

"In that case," argued Dan, "we wouldn't have to follow the brown rascals on foot. We could use the ship to follow 'em, and land and fight where we found 'em."

"To be sure," Ensign Darrin agreed. "But the Mexicans, knowing their own swamps, would have considerable advantage. They might have part of their force retreat, drawing us further and further into a swamp, and then have another force get between us and our ships."

"Let 'em try it," retorted Dan Dalzell, grimly, "If there is anything new that the Greasers want to know about American methods of fighting, our fleet is full of officers who are willing to be patient instructors. But take my word for it, Dave, if the Mexicans ever try to draw us into one of those swamps, they'll learn so much about real Yankee fighting that it will be fatal to all the Mexicans who take the instruction from us!"

"That's all very good," Darrin nodded, thoughtfully. "Still, we shall make a greater success of operations in the swamps if we study them as much as possible at present."

"I hope the study will soon be followed by a recitation," grinned Dalzell. "I feel that I'm going stale with so much study. Now, if we could only hear a few shots, and then fall in with an advancing firing line!"

"You bloodthirsty wretch!" rebuked Ensign Darrin, but he smiled in sympathy.

"This waiting and watching grows wearisome," groaned Danny Grin.

"But we're watching behind big guns," returned Dave Darrin, grimly. "Surely, when our ships are down here in such force, and others are being rushed through preparation before coming into these waters, there must be something more in the air than the ordinary kind of watching and waiting. Cheer up, Dan! Before long you'll hear some of our big guns speak, and you'll hear the rattle of small arms, too."

"Understand, please," begged Dalzell, "I'm not bloodthirsty, and I abhor the very thought of war, but, since we're doing all the watching and waiting, I wish these Mexicans would hurry up and start something!"

Trent climbed to the superstructure. Then, catching sight of his juniors, he came toward them.

"What are you doing?" he asked.

"Watching," sighed Dave.

"And waiting," added Danny Grin.

"Then perhaps you youngsters will be interested in the news of what's going on under this superstructure," suggested Lieutenant Trent.

"What's happening below?" demanded Dalzell. "More watching—-and waiting?"

"Why, I have an idea that we won't have to wait much longer," replied Trent, smiling at the eager faces before him. "I've just learned that, for the last twenty minutes, Captain Gales has been standing in the wireless room, and that Commander Bainbridge is with him. They are, so I hear, having a hot and heavy wireless talk with Admiral Fletcher."

"A little *talk*, as a relief from so much watching and waiting, eh?" asked Darrin, dryly.

"Why, I believe that the talk is going to lead to something real," replied Lieutenant Trent, trying hard to keep the flash of excitement from showing in his own eyes. "The fact is, something has happened."

"Don't 'string' us like that!" urged Danny Grin. "Why, Trent, the American Navy, and the Army, too, has been waiting for three years or more for something to happen. But so far it has all happened on the Mexican side. Don't tell us, at this late day, that the United States is going to start anything to happening on the other side."

"There's something up," Trent insisted. "I don't know what it is; I haven't an idea of the nature of the happening, but of this I feel rather sure,—-that now, at last, the Mexicans have done something that will turn Yankee guns and Yankee men loose."

"I wonder if you're any good as a prophet, Trent?" pondered Dan, studying his division officer's face keenly.

"We'll wait and see," laughed the lieutenant. "If there really is anything in the wind, I think we'll have a suspicion of what it is by mess-hour to-night. A little more watching and waiting won't hurt us."

"Hear that commotion on the quarter-deck?" demanded Dave, suddenly. "I hear a lot of talking there. Come on. We'll see if *waiting* is about to be turned into *doing*."

Trent walked slowly aft. Still chatting with him, Dave and Dan kept by his side. Then they stood looking down upon the quarter-deck.

Presently two messengers came running out, looking eagerly about them. One messenger, catching sight of the three officers on the superstructure, came bounding up the steps, halting and saluting.

"Compliments of the executive officer," announced the messenger; "Ensigns Darrin and Dalzell are directed to report to his office immediately."

"Perhaps you'll hear the news at once," murmured Trent, as his juniors left him.

When the two ensigns reported to him, Commander Bainbridge was pacing the passageway outside his office.

"The captain is awaiting us in his office," said the executive.
"We will go there at once."

The instant he entered the captain's quarters, Darrin had sudden misgivings of some impending misfortune, for Lieutenant Cantor, very erect, and looking both stern and important, was talking in low tones with Captain Gales.

"Now, what has the scoundrel found to fasten upon me?" Ensign Dave Darrin wondered, with a start. "And how has he managed to drag Dan into it?"

CHAPTER VI

"Gentlemen," began Captain Gales, seriously, though there was a pleasant smile on his face, "I imagine I have extremely pleasant news for two of you. Commander Bainbridge and Lieutenant Trent have already some idea of the news, but I will go over it again for the benefit of all here."

"I may go on breathing again," Dave thought grimly. "Then this communication can hardly be in reference to any complaint that Cantor may have lodged against me."

"Messrs. Cantor, Darrin and Dalzell will tonight," resumed the captain, "lead the first expeditions by United States forces that have been made in a great many years."

Had war been declared? Both Dave and Dan fairly jumped with eagerness.

"A letter, coming by some mysterious, round-about route," continued Captain Gales, "has reached the American consul at Vera Cruz. An American party, consisting of Mr. and Mrs. John Carmody and two small sons, and of Mrs. Sarah Deeming and two daughters nineteen and sixteen years of age, came down by muleback from the plateau some three weeks ago. Carmody is a planter up in that part of the country, and the Deemings were his guests. Different bands of bandit raiders have visited the Carmody plantation from time to time within the last two years, stealing stock and supplies, and levying money blackmail, until Carmody found himself practically ruined, unless the present crops should turn out well.

"Three weeks ago Carmody learned that it was high time for isolated Americans to reach the protection of some large town. Attended by two peons (native laborers), and travelling on mule back, the party started through the mountains for Vera Cruz. Four hours out from the plantation the party was halted by a score of men led by a brigand named Cosetta, who is reported to be the right hand man of the notorious Zapata himself.

"Cosetta, it appears, believed that he could force Carmody to pay a large indemnity, in money, for the release of himself and family and their woman friends. First of all, the Americans were taken to a house near a deserted sugar mill, somewhere on the coast opposite us. This sugar mill stands on a lagoon, and that is as much of a description as Carmody could furnish in his hastily penned letter. But we know that there are, along this part of the coast, three such deserted sugar mills, each standing on a lagoon.

"Plainly, the Carmodys must be in the house near one of these three mills, but which one it is we cannot even guess. Admiral Fletcher sent me the news two hours ago, by wireless. Ever since then we have been in earnest communication upon the subject, and now I have my orders in the matter."

"It would be possible, of course, for us to visit each one of these lagoons in turn. However, if we visited the wrong mill first, these bandits undoubtedly have some means of signaling to comrades. Our landing party might be observed, and the news of the attempt at rescue would be signaled by fires or otherwise, and the discovery of our designs would undoubtedly result in the Carmody party being butchered at once.

"Acting under the orders of Cosetta, or, I might say, under his threats, Mr. Carmody has sent appeals in every direction he could think of for the funds to pay the hundred thousand dollar ransom demanded for the party. These requests have been carried on through agents of Cosetta, but none of the appeals have borne fruit. Wearied, Cosetta has announced that on a certain morning, if the ransom has not arrived, Carmody and all the members of his party, even including the children, shall be shot and buried in hidden graves. There is little doubt that Cosetta will carry out his threat, and to-morrow morning is the time set for this wholesale murder."

Fire flashed in the eyes of the Navy officers who heard this announcement.

"As you may be certain," continued Captain Gales, "Admiral Fletcher has wired me that this proposed atrocity must be prevented, and the American captives rescued at all hazards. Now, attend me while I show you the detail chart for this part of the coast."

Captain Gales turned to his desk, where the map was spread.

"Here, as you will see," he continued, "is a sugar mill belonging to the Alvarez plantations. Ten miles to the eastward of the Alvarez mill is the Perdita mill; ten miles to the westward of the Alvarez mill is the Acunda mill. To-night there will be no moon. At nine o'clock we shall lie to off the Alvarez mill, and three sixty-foot launches will be lowered to the water. Lieutenant Cantor will command one of these launches, Ensign Darrin another and Ensign Dalzell the third. Each launch will carry one automatic gun, and a landing party of a corporal, six marines, a petty officer and twelve seamen. Each party will be armed, but, gentlemen, I must caution you as to the extreme seriousness of any conflict on shore, or of firing, even though your fire is not directed at human beings. These are days when our relations with Mexico are of an extremely delicate nature. If we send an armed party on shore, and its members fight, it will be difficult, indeed, for our government to make the claim that an act of war was not committed on the soil of a nation that is, at present, at peace with us. The consequences of a fight are likely to be grave indeed. Therefore, the officer in command of each landing party is especially warned that the rescue of the American prisoners must be accomplished by strategy, not by fighting."

Captain Gales looked keenly at each of the three young officers concerned, to make sure that they understood the full gravity of the situation.

"Strategy, remember—-not fighting," Captain Gales repeated. "Now, the 'Long Island' will not go within four miles of the coast. Yet, despite the darkness to-night, it is likely that a craft as large as this ship would be noted from the shore, and her errand suspected. That might result in the execution of the American captives before aid could reach them. So, when we reach a point opposite the Alvarez mill, Lieutenant Cantor's launch will be put over the side first, while the ship continues under slow headway."

Lieutenant Cantor will lie to, while the other two launches are being lowered. Ensigns Darrin and Dalzell will then steam back and report to Lieutenant Cantor. Under slow speed it will take the launches, commanded by the two ensigns, each about an hour and ten minutes to reach their respective lagoon destinations. It will take the lieutenant just under thirty minutes to reach the Alvarez lagoon. Ensign Dalzell will go to the Perdita lagoon, and Ensign Darrin to the Acunda lagoon. Forty minutes after Dalzell and Darrin have steamed away, Lieutenant Cantor will run in to the Alvarez mill. Our launches are not likely to be observed from shore, where the 'Long Island,' if she remained in these waters, would be sure to be seen and recognized.

"Therefore, after dropping the steamers, we shall go ahead at cruising speed and not return opposite the Alvarez mill until called by a rocket, which Lieutenant Cantor will send up as soon as the rescue has been accomplished —or has failed. But, gentlemen"—-here Captain Gales' voice sank low, yet vibrated with intense earnestness—"all of you will realize the extreme importance of your mission, and the awful consequences of failure. Therefore, I feel certain that none of you will break the Navy's long list of traditions for zealous, careful, successful performance of duty. Lieutenant Cantor will be in command of the expedition, as a whole."

For some minutes the officers remained in the captain's quarters, discussing further the important work of the coming night.

As no instructions for secrecy had been asked or expected, Commander Bainbridge soon told the news to a few of the "Long Island's" ranking officers, who, in turn passed it on.

"Of all the luck that some officers have!" groaned Lieutenant Trent, as he passed Dave Darrin. "How did you work it, Darrin, to secure one of the details for to-night that any subordinate officer on this ship would have been delighted to see come his way?"

"I don't know," Dave laughingly admitted.

"Darrin, are you hard up?" asked Lieutenant Holton, five minutes later.

"I have a few dollars left," Dave smiled.

"If you can get me shifted to your detail for to-night I'll reward you with a month of my pay," promised the lieutenant.

"Thank you," Dave smiled, gravely. "Even if the change could be easily arranged, I'm afraid I wouldn't give up my chance for six months' pay."

"No chance for me, then," sighed Holton. "I can't remember that I ever had six months' of my pay together at one time."

"Darrin," exclaimed Lieutenant Commander Denton, still a little later, "I never realized that you had so much impudence! The idea of a mere ensign leading such an expedition ashore to-night! I wanted that myself."

"I am not at all sure that my performance will be one of glory," smiled Darrin.

"It won't, if Cantor can manage to queer you in any way," murmured Denton to himself, as he moved on.

In the ward-room that evening the "impertinence" of two new ensigns in capturing such prized details was commented upon with a great deal of chaffing. Even Lieutenant Cantor was declared to be much too young to be entrusted with such important work.

At eight o'clock the fortunate lieutenant and ensigns were once more sent for, to go over the map and instructions with Captain Gales.

At nine o'clock, just before the "*Long Island*" was abreast of the Alvarez mill, the first launch was cleared away and lowered, falling behind and lying to.

Then Darrin, with his own crew, went down over the side to the launch towing alongside. It was Coxswain Riley who stood by to catch the young commanding officer's arm.

"Hullo, Coxswain," was Dave's greeting. "Are you to handle the launch to-night?"

"No, sir," Riley answered, saluting. "I am the petty officer in charge of the seamen. Coxswain Schmidt handles the launch, sir."

As soon as his party had hurried aboard, Darrin gave the order to cast off. Under slow speed astern the launch joined Lieutenant Cantor's craft.

"I'm glad that I'm to have you on shore tonight with me, Coxswain," said Dave, heartily.

"Thank you, sir," answered the coxswain, saluting and actually blushing with pleasure.

Soon after Dan's launch ranged up with the other two, and the "*Long Island*" was vanishing in the distance ahead, not a light showing, for it is the privilege of the commander of a war vessel to sail without lights, when the interests of the services may be furthered thereby. Nor did any of the launches display lights.

As each of the boats was to run at slow speed, it was hoped that each landing party would reach shore without detection.

Lieutenant Cantor went over the instructions once more, talking in low tones across the water.

"And above all, remember that there is to be no fighting," Cantor added, impressively, looking straight into Darrin's eyes.

"Punk orders, when each man is provided with a hundred rounds of rifle ammunition, and when each automatic gun is supplied with two thousand rounds!" grumbled Coxswain Riley, under his breath.

"Gentlemen, you will now get under way," ordered Lieutenant Cantor. "You will remember each sentence of your instructions!"

Silently, two of the launches stole away into the night, bound east and west, while the third launch awaited the time to start shoreward.

On Darrin's launch there was little talking, and that in whispers. Dave had made a most careful study of the map, and felt certain that he could give the course straight into the lagoon on which the Acunda mill stood.

"Coxswain Schmidt," said Ensign Darrin, in a low voice, when still some four miles away from the proposed place of landing, "when you are close enough to shore to signal the engineer, you will do so by hand signal, not by use of the bell. Seaman Berne will watch for your signals, and convey them to the engineer."

"Very good, sir," replied both coxswain and seaman.

"Probably it won't be my luck to find the American captives at the Acunda plantation," murmured Darrin.

None the less, when he at last sighted the lagoon, his heart began to beat excitedly.

Under reduced speed, now, the launch stole into the lagoon. Less than a quarter of a mile from shore the sugar mill, deserted since the rebellion first took acute form, stood out dimly against the dark sky.

To within a hundred and fifty yards of the mill the launch ran, then swung in at a nearly ruined old wharf.

Ensign Dave Darrin was first to step ashore, signing to his men to follow him with all stealth.

"Corporal," Darrin whispered, "unless summoned later, you will stand by the launch with your men, to prevent it being rushed in case the bandits are abroad to-night. Coxswain Riley, you will form your men loosely and follow me, keeping about a hundred yards to the rear, making no sound as you advance."

Officer and men were all in dark uniforms, which in the blackness of the night would not be seen at any distance, whereas the white tropical uniforms would have immediately betrayed the raiders.

About seven hundred feet beyond the sugar mill Darrin had already located the house. Like the old mill, the residence was in darkness. Not a light shone, nor was there a sound to be heard.

"This eerie stretch of ground makes one think of a graveyard," thought Darrin, with a comical little shiver, as his left hand gripped his sword scabbard tightly to prevent it clanking against his left heel.

He turned to look behind him. Riley and twelve armed seamen were following him like so many unsubstantial spectres.

Past the mill, and down the road to the house strode Darrin, but his moving feet made hardly a sound.

A little before the house ran a line of flowering tropical hedge. Darrin gained this, and was about to pass in through an opening in the hedge when a figure suddenly appeared in the darkness right ahead of him.

A rifle was leveled at the young ensign's breast, and in a steady voice came the hail that set the young ensign's heart to beating fast:

"*Quien vive*"

It was the Spanish challenge—-"Who goes there?"

CHAPTER VII

DAVE DARRIN TO THE RESCUE

Dave's sword hung at his side. His revolver was in its scabbard over his left hip, but just out of view of the sentry.

As to his being in uniform, he realized that the night was so dark that there was little danger of his nationality being discovered.

All these thoughts flashed through his mind in a twinkling, as they should with a good officer.

Darrin's course of action was as swiftly decided.

"Amigo," he replied, tranquilly. "Amigo de los prisoneros!" (Friends of the prisoners).

By the time the second explanation had left his lips Dave had bounded forward, struck aside the rifle, and had gripped the sentry by the throat, bearing him to the ground.

A blow from one of the young ensign's fists, and the fellow lay still.

Espying trouble from the rear, Coxswain Riley started his men on a swift run toward the spot. In a few moments the sentry, doubtless badly scared, had been gagged, and bound hand and foot with the handy hitches of jack tars.

"Leave him there," Darrin directed in an undertone. "Coxswain, post eight men around the house, and take command of them. I will take the other four men with me."

Swiftly Darrin led his little squad around to the rear of the house, since the front was closed and dark.

A doorway stood open, showing a room lighted by two candles that stood on a table. Around the table were seven men, eating and drinking. Plainly they had not heard the brief scuffle at the front.

With a nod to his four men Darrin led the way inside. Instantly the seven men were on their feet, staring wildly at the intruders. One man started for a stack of rifles that stood in a corner, but Ensign Darrin hurled him back.

"Don't let any man reach for a gun, or draw any sort of weapon," Darrin ordered, quickly.

Then to the Mexicans, in Spanish, Dave shouted:

"Stand where you are, and no harm will be done to you. We have not come here to molest you, but you hold Americans prisoners here, and we mean to take them away with us."

"No, no," answered one of the Mexicans, smilingly, "you are mistaken. We have no prisoners here."

Dave's heart sank within him for one brief moment. Had he made a mistake in invading this house, only to find that his mission was to be fruitless?

Then he suspected Mexican treachery.

"Pardon me," he urged in Spanish, "if I satisfy myself that you are telling the truth. Stand where you are, all of you, and no harm shall come to you. But don't make the mistake of moving or of reaching for weapons."

Darrin strode swiftly past the group and stepped into a hallway, in which were stairs leading above.

"Are there any Americans here," he shouted, "who want help? If so, there are American sailors here ready to give aid."

From above there came a single exclamation of joy, followed by a scurrying of feet.

From above sounded a voice demanding in Spanish:

"Shall I let the prisoners go?"

"You will have to," answered the same voice that had answered Dave. "We are attacked by *los marineros Americanos*." (American sailors).

For the men in the other room now knew that there were more than these four seamen at hand. As soon as he heard voices inside Riley had cleverly caused his men to walk about the house with heavy tread, and the Mexicans believed themselves to be outnumbered.

"Is it true that there are American sailors below?" called a man's husky voice.

"A detachment from the United States Navy, sir," Dave replied, gleefully. "Are you Mr. Carmody?"

"Yes, yes!"

"Then bring down your party. We have force enough to resist any attempt to hold you, and if any harm is offered you, we shall avenge it. Shall I come upstairs for you, Mr. Carmody?"

"If you don't mind," answered the voice of the man above. "There are two guards up here who seem undecided whether to shoot us or to let us pass."

Instantly Ensign Darrin ran to the stairs, mounting them. Yet he was careful to take no chance of being surprised in the dark, for he well understood the treachery of the natives with whom he had to deal.

However, Darrin reached the landing unattacked. Down the hallway he saw an open door, through which a dim light shone. Before the door were two Mexicans, each armed with a rifle.

"You will permit the American party to pass," Dave commanded, bluntly, in the best Spanish that he had learned at Annapolis.

One of the sentries again called out loudly, demanding instructions from below.

"You will have to let the prisoners pass," came from downstairs.

At that both sentries moved away from the door.

"Will you be good enough to come out?" Darrin called, keeping his eye on the two guards, who stood glowering sullenly at him. He had not drawn his revolver, and did not wish to do so.

The door was cautiously opened and a man's head appeared. One look at Dave and the door was flung wide by a tall, serious-eyed man whose hair was gray at the temples.

"Come," he called to those behind him. "I see the uniform of our own Navy. I never paid much attention to it before, but at thus moment it's the most welcome sight in the world."

Head erect, shoulders thrown back, an expression of deep gratitude in his eyes, John Carmody stepped out into the hallway.

Behind him was a middle-aged woman, followed by two pretty girls. Then came another woman, younger than the first, who led two boys, one of four years, the other of six.

"I was sent here," Dave announced, cap in hand, "to find and rescue John Carmody, his wife and two sons, and a Mrs. Deeming and her two daughters."

"We are they," Mr. Carmody declared.

"Do you know of any other prisoners, Americans or otherwise, who are held here by the bandits, sir?" Ensign Darrin inquired.

"I do not know of any other captives here," replied Mr. Carmody, promptly. "In fact, I do not believe there are any others."

"Mr. Carmody, if you will lead your party down the stairs and through the hallway to the room at the end of the passage, I will bring up the rear of this little American procession."

Mr. Carmody obeyed without hesitation. One after another the trembling women followed, Mrs. Carmody leading her two young sons.

Out in the hallway Mr. Carmody caught sight of the sailors, who stood revealed in the light of the room, as with watchful eyes they held the seven Mexicans at bay.

"Mr. Carmody," called Dave, just before he entered that room, "I will ask you to lead your party out of doors. You will find other American sailors there, sir."

Entering the room, Dave stood, cap still in hand, until the last of the American women had passed into the open. Then, replacing his cap, the young naval officer turned to the Mexican who had spoken to the others and who now stood sullenly eyeing the sailors.

"I have carried out my orders," Dave declared, in Spanish. "I regret that I have no authority to punish you as you deserve. Instead, therefore, I will wish you good night."

Signing to his sailors to pass out before him, Dave was the last to leave the room. All four of the young sailors, however, stood just outside, where their rifles might sweep the room, at need, until their officer had passed out.

"Hicks," called Dave, to one of the party of sailors who had surrounded the house, "lead these people to the water. The rest of us will bring up the rear."

Seeing the women and children of his party under safe guidance, Mr. Carmody turned back to speak to their rescuer.

"Sir," asked the older man, "did you know that, on account of the failure to raise the ransom money, we were all, even the babies, to be put to death at sunrise?"

"Yes, sir," Dave nodded.

"Then perhaps you are able to understand the gratitude to which I shall endeavor to give some expression as soon as we are in a place of safety."

"It is not my wish to hear expressions of gratitude, Mr. Carmody," Dave Darrin answered. "As to safety, however, I fancy we are safe enough already."

Mr. Carmody shook his head energetically.

"We have twenty men to the nine we saw in that house," Dave smiled. "Surely they will not endeavor to attack us."

"Cosetta, the bandit, was he to whom you spoke in the house," replied John

48

Carmody. "He has but a few men in the house, but there are twenty or thirty more sleeping in the stables behind the house. Altogether, unless he has sent some away, he must have more than sixty men hereabouts."

"Then we must go on the double quick to our boat," returned Darrin. "Hicks," he called down the straggling line, which was now just outside the grounds and headed toward the mill, "keep the whole party moving as rapidly as possible."

Yet Darrin was not afraid for himself, for he halted while the party hastened forward, scanning the darkness to his rear. Seeing the ensign standing there alone, Riley and half a dozen sailors came running back.

"I'm afraid you're headed the wrong way, Riley," smiled Dave. "I hear there is a large force behind us, and we must embark as rapidly as possible."

"It won't take us long to tumble into the launch, sir," the coxswain replied, doggedly, "but we won't leave our officer behind. We couldn't think of doing it."

"Not even under orders?" Darrin inquired.

"We'd hate to disobey orders, sir," Riley mumbled, looking rather abashed, "but——-"

"Hark!" called Dave, holding up a hand.

Back of the flowering hedge he heard the swift patter of bare feet.

Out of the darkness came a flash of a pistol shot. It was answered instantly by a ragged but crashing volley.

Long tongues of flame spat out into the night. The air was full of whistling bullets.

Pseu! pss-seu! pss-seu! Sang the steel-jacketed bullets about the ears of the Americans.

Then the sailor nearest Ensign Dave Darrin fell to the ground with a stifled gasp.

CHAPTER VIII

DISOBEDIENCE OF ORDERS

Outnumbered, the Americans did not falter.

Save for Hicks, the guide, and the wounded man, the sailors threw themselves automatically to one knee, bringing their rifles to "ready."

For a moment Ensign Darrin felt sick at heart. He was under orders not to fire, to employ no armed force in a way that might be construed as an act of war in the country of another nation.

Yet here were his men being fired upon, one already wounded, and American women and children in danger of losing their lives.

Perhaps it was against orders, as given, but the real military commander is sometimes justified in disregarding orders.

At the first sound of shots all of the sailors, except Hicks, came running back, crouching close to earth. As soon as they reached the thin little line the men knelt and waited breathlessly. Dave's resolution was instantly taken. Though he might hang for his disobedience of orders, he would not tamely submit to seeing his men shot down ruthlessly.

Still less would he permit American women and children to be endangered.

Orders, or no orders——-

"Ready, men!" he shouted, above the sharp reports of the Cosetta rifle fire. "Aim low at the hedge! Fire at will!"

Cr-r-r-rack! rang out the American Navy rifles.

Filled with the fighting enthusiasm of the moment, Darrin drew his automatic revolver, firing ten shots swiftly at different points along the hedge.

From behind that screen came cries of pain, for the Mexican is an excitable individual, who does not take his wounds with the calmness evinced by an American.

Another American sailor had dropped. John Carmody, who had remained with the defending party, snatched up one of the rifles. Standing, he rushed in a magazine full of bullets, then bent to help himself to more from the belt of the rifle's former carrier.

Fitting his revolver with a fresh load of cartridges, Dave held his fire for any emergency that might arise.

A marine dashed up, nearly out of breath.

"Sir," panted the marine, "Corporal Ross wants to know if you want to order the Colt gun and the marines up here."

"No," Dave decided instantly. "Help one of our wounded men back to the launch and tell Corporal Ross to remain where he is. Is the Colt loaded and ashore?"

"Yes, sir; ready for instant action."

"Did Hicks get the women and children to the launch?"

"No sir; he has hidden them behind the lower end of the sugar mill. The air is too full of bullets to expose the women to them."

"Good for Hicks! Tell him I said so. He is to remain where he is until either the Mexicans' fire ceases or he receives different orders from me."

"Very good, sir."

Stooping, the marine picked up the worse injured of the two wounded sailors and swiftly bore him away in his arms.

"Cease firing!" shouted Darrin, running along his valiant little line of sailors. "Load your magazines and let the rifles cool until the Mexicans start up again."

For, with the exception of a shot here and there from behind the hedge, the destructive fire had ceased.

"We must have hit a few of them," chuckled Darrin to John Carmody, who stood beside him.

"I hope you killed them all," replied the planter. "They're brutes, when they have their own way."

"Riley!"

"Aye, aye, sir."

"Pass the word to the men and we'll slip back. I don't like the silence behind the hedge. I suspect that the men have been withdrawn and that we are to be flanked below the sugar mill. Tell the men to fall back by rushes, not returning any fire unless ordered."

"Aye, aye, sir."

A moment later ten jackies were retreating. They gained the sugar mill, and passed it.

"Hicks," called Ensign Darrin, "get your party aboard. Run for it!"

"Aye, aye, sir."

"And help this wounded man back to the launch."

The sailor, who had been carrying the second wounded man, turned him over to Hicks, who carried his burden manfully.

Dave continued to retreat more slowly with his fighting force, taking frequent observations rearward. From the hedge a few, sniping shots came now and then, but, as no one was hit, Darrin did not allow the fire to be returned.

Suddenly, three hundred yards away, a volley crashed out on the right.

"Flanked!" muttered Darrin, grimly, as Riley threw his men into line to meet the new attack. "I expected it. Aim two feet above the ground, men, and fire at will until you have emptied your magazines twice."

Down by the launch, and not thirty feet from the wharf, stood Corporal Ross with his marines and the Colt machine gun. The marines were wild to join in the firing, but would not do so until ordered. Darrin was loath to let them draw the enemy's fire until the women had been made as safe as possible on the launch.

As the American firing ceased, Dave called the order:

"Load magazines, but reserve fire. Rush three hundred feet closer to the wharf and then halt and form again."

This move was carried out, but a third sailor dropped wounded.

As a lull came in the firing, Ensign Darrin blew a signal on his whistle. In response, two marines came sprinting to the spot.

"Take this wounded man to the launch," Darrin ordered.

"Corporal Ross hopes, sir, you'll soon give him leave to turn the machine gun loose," one of the marines suggested respectfully.

"I'll give the order as soon as the time comes," Darrin promised. "Tell Corporal Ross that one flash from my pocket lamp will mean 'open fire,' and that two flashes will mean 'cease firing.'

"Very good, sir."

The wounded man was borne away. Again Dave attempted a rush, then reformed his men, this time not more than two hundred and fifty feet from the stern of the launch.

"Riley!"

"Aye, aye, sir!"

"You will take command here. I must see to the safety of our passengers."

"Aye, aye, sir."

"Fire when you think best, but do not let the men waste ammunition. We have but a hundred rounds apiece."

"I know it, sir."

Then Dave dashed down to the wharf, just before which stood Corporal Ross looking the picture of disappointment. He had hoped for permission to open fire.

Ensign Darrin and John Carmody ran to the launch together. Aided by Coxswain Schmidt, Hicks had done his work well, placing the women and children flat along the bottom of the craft, where they were little likely to be found by flying bullets.

Again the fire had slackened. Dave stood with the marines, peering into the blackness beyond.

"Can't you call in your party and make a quick dash down the lagoon?" inquired John Carmody, approaching, a rifle still gripped by one hand and a cartridge-belt thrown over one shoulder.

"We can't travel fast in the lagoon, sir," Dave answered, "and Cosetta's men can run as fast along the shore, keeping up a fire that would be more deadly when we're crowded together aboard the launch. I want to silence the scoundrel's fire, if possible, before we try the dash out into the Gulf."

"You appear to have discouraged the men who flanked you," said Mr. Carmody, looking towards the shore.

"Yes, sir; but, judging by the rifle flashes there were not more than twenty men in that flanking party. We still have to hear from another body, and I believe they are hiding in the mill, ready to snipe us from there. Besides, probably a smaller party has been sent from the flankers to lie in wait and get us as we go through the lagoon. It's a bad trap, Mr. Carmody, and we must move slowly, if we wish to get away with our lives."

While they stood watching, Riley's handful of men came running to the spot.

At the same moment shots rang out from the roof of the sugar mill.

"There we are!" Darrin exclaimed. "And men on a roof are the hardest to hit."

In a jiffy a yell rose from the flankers, who now rose and came charging forward across some four hundred feet of intervening space.

"Give 'em the Colt, Corporal!" Ensign Darrin roared.

There was a yell of rage from the Mexicans as the machine gun barked forth. With the muzzle describing an arc of several degrees, many of the flankers were hit. The others threw themselves flat on the ground to escape its destructive fire.

From the mill another score of charging Mexicans had started, yelling in Spanish:

"Death to the Gringos."

Leaping forward, Darrin felt a sudden sting of pain in his right foot. A bullet, sent in low, had ripped the sole of his shoe, inflicting a painful wound.

"Cease firing, Corporal!" Dave ordered, hobbling to the machine gun. "Swing her nose around. Now, give it to 'em."

As the machine gun barked forth again the raiders from the mill found good excuse for halting. There are times when a machine gun is worth a battalion of infantry.

Yet one bullet is enough to kill a man. A marine fell at Dave's feet. The young ensign bent over him; one look was enough to prove that this defender of his countrymen was dead.

As the fire from the machine gun ceased, a wild cheer rose on the air. Now, from four different points groups of Mexicans rose and charged, firing as they ran.

One desperate dash, and they would overwhelm the crippled little Navy party.

Defeat for Dave Darrin's command meant the massacre of all the survivors of his rescue party, and of the American men and women in their care!

Ensign Dave Darrin realized this with a sickening heart.

CHAPTER IX

CANTOR FINDS HIS CHANCE

Prompt action alone could save the women and children who lay cowering in the launch.

"Corporal, kneel with your men, and let them have it as fast as you can!" ordered Dave. "Riley, get your men into the boat, and take the Colt with you. Post it as fast as you can on the starboard quarter!"

Dave himself stood behind the kneeling marines, a fair target for every hostile bullet.

John Carmody, too, felt in honor bound to risk himself beside the young Navy ensign.

"All sea-going, sir!" called Coxswain Riley. "Schmidt, make ready to cast off," sang back Darrin.

Now the different groups of Mexicans, who had been halted for a minute under the brisk fire, saw their prey slipping away from them.

With yells of fury, Cosetta's men rose and attempted the final charge.

"Marines aboard!" yelled Darrin.

Almost in the same instant, loaded revolver in hand, Dave sprang to the gunwale and landed on the after deck.

Without waiting for the order from his chief, Schmidt cast off, with the aid of the single sailor under his own command. The engineer went ahead at slow speed for a few seconds while Riley steered the launch clear of the wharf and headed for deeper, safer water.

"Half speed ahead!" shouted Darrin, as Schmidt sprang to the wheel, while Riley, snatching up his rifle, joined the fighting men. Uttering howls of rage as they saw their prey escaping them, the Mexicans rushed out onto the wharf in a mad attempt to board before it was too late.

Three men would have succeeded in boarding the launch, had they not been shot down as they leaped for the after deck.

"Give it to them with the Colt, Corporal!" Dave called. "Every other man fire with his rifle!"

Before he had finished speaking, the reloaded Colt belched forth its rain of death. It was the machine gun, with its muzzle swiftly turning in an arc of a circle that did the most execution among the outlaws, but the riflemen did their share.

Until his rifle barrel was too hot to hold in his hands, John Carmody shot rapidly, yet coolly putting into his work all the pent-up indignation that he had felt for days against Cosetta and his men.

"Stop the gun!" ordered Dave Darrin, resting a hand on the shoulder of the marine corporal. "Don't waste its fire."

The launch was now free of the shore, and moving down the lagoon at half speed. On the wharf fully a score of Mexicans either lay dead or dying.

Dave's spoken order to the engineer caused the launch to increase its speed.

"Line up at the starboard rail," Dave called to the men grouped about him. "We're going to catch it from the shore."

The launch was a few hundred yards down the lagoon when Darrin, alertly watching, made out several figures on the eastern shore.

Patiently he waited until the first flash from a rifle was seen, which was followed instantly by the report and the "pss-seu!" of a bullet.

"Let 'em have the rest of what's in the Colt," the young ensign directed, calmly. "Men, don't fire too rapidly, but keep up your work. We want to be remembered by Cosetta, if he has the good luck to be still alive."

It was neither a heavy nor an accurate fire that came now from the enraged Mexicans. Helped out by the Colt, the fire from the moving craft was sharp enough to discourage the rapidly diminishing ardor of the miscreants on shore.

Just as the launch rounded the point of land at the mouth of the lagoon, and stood out into open water at full speed, a stray bullet killed Seaman Hicks.

"Yes, sir, he's dead, poor fellow!" exclaimed Riley, looking up as Ensign Dave stepped hastily forward for a look at his man. "Hicks was a fine sailor too."

"For a party that wasn't expected to fight," returned Darrin wearily, "we've had a pretty big casualty list—-two killed, and three wounded."

"You're wounded yourself, sir," exclaimed Riley.

"Oh, my boot was cut," Darrin assented, indifferently.

"Look at your wrist, sir," urged the young Coxswain.

Dave glanced down at his left wrist, to find it covered with blood.

"It must look worse than it is," Darrin commented, listlessly. "I didn't even feel it."

"It will need attention, sir, just the same," Riley urged. "Let me fix it up, sir, with a first aid bandage."

There was a water cask aboard. As the launch was now out of close range, and the Mexicans had apparently given up firing, Riley brought a cup of water, poured it over the wrist, and wiped away the blood.

"A scratch, as I thought," smiled Dave. "Not even enough to get excused from watch duty."

"You'll have it dressed, sir, won't you, as soon as you get aboard the '*Long Island*' again?" urged Riley, applying the sterilized bandage with swift skill. "If the scoundrels used any of the brass-jacketed bullets of which they're so fond, a scratch like that might lead to blood poisoning, sir."

In a few minutes more the launch was out of rifle range. Dave ordered the course changed to east by north-east, in order to reach the rendezvous of the three launches.

"Steamer ahead, sir!" sang out the bow lookout, a few minutes later.

"Whereaway?" called Darrin, moving forward.

"Three points off starboard bow, sir," replied the sailorman. "It looks like our own launch, sir."

By this time Darrin was well forward. He peered closely at the approaching craft, for she might be a Mexican Federal gunboat that had fallen into the hands of rebels or outlaws.

"It's our own launch," pronounced Darrin, a minute later. He reached for the whistle pull and blew three blasts of welcome, which were promptly answered.

The two craft now neared each other. "Launch ahoy, there!" called a voice from the bow of the other craft.

"Aye, aye, sir!" Darrin answered.

"Is that you, Ensign Darrin?"

"Aye, aye, sir."

"Lay to. I am coming alongside."

As the launch under Dave's command lost headway, then lay idly on the light ground swell, the other launch circled about her, then came up under the port quarter.

"Did you find the American party, Ensign Darrin?" demanded Lieutenant Cantor.

"Yes, sir; I have the entire party aboard and uninjured."

"Was there any trouble?" asked Cantor.

"Yes, sir. We were fired upon, and forced to defend ourselves."

"You fired upon the natives?" exclaimed Lieutenant Cantor, in an \ astonished tone.

"I had to, sir."

"In the face of orders not to fight?" pressed Dave's enemy.

"Sir, if I had not fought, I would have lost my entire command," Darrin answered, with an indignation that he could not completely veil.

"Ensign Darrin," came the sharp rebuke,

"You have disobeyed the orders of Captain Gales, which were repeated by me just before we parted company. Did your fire hit any of the Mexicans?"

"I think we must have done so, sir," Dave returned dryly. "Several of them lay down, at all events."

"Any losses in your own command?" pressed Cantor.

"Two men killed and four wounded."

"The consequences of disobedience of orders, sir!" cried Lieutenant Cantor, angrily. "Ensign Darrin, I am certain that you should not have been entrusted with the command of a launch."

"That sounds like a reflection on the Captain's judgment, sir!"
Dave rejoined, rather warmly.

"No unnecessary remarks," thundered Cantor. "I shall not place you in arrest, but on our return to the ship I shall report at once your flagrant disobedience of orders."

Darrin did not answer, but the hot blood now surged to his head, suffusing his cheeks. He was deeply humiliated.

"Young man, if you call that good sense," rumbled the deep voice of John Carmody, "then I don't agree with you. You condemn Darrin———"

"Who is speaking?" roared Lieutenant Cantor.

"My name is John Carmody," returned the planter, coolly.

"Then be good enough to remain silent," commanded Cantor.

"Since I'm on a government boat," retorted the planter, "I suppose I may as well do as I'm ordered. But at some other time I shall air my opinion of you, young man, as freely as I please."

Lieutenant Cantor bit his lips, then gave the order to proceed to the appointed rendezvous.

As Cantor's launch neared Dalzell's steamer, the lieutenant ordered a rocket sent up. From away over on the horizon an answering rocket was seen.

Forty minutes later the "*Long Island*" lay to close by. Cantor's launch was the first to go in alongside.

"Were you successful?" hailed the voice of the executive officer from the bridge.

"Ensign Darrin was, sir," Cantor replied, through the megaphone.

"Are all the missing Americans safe?"

"Yes, sir," Cantor continued.

"And all our own men?"

"Two killed, sir, and four wounded, through what I believe to be disobedience of orders."

Instructions came for Lieutenant Cantor's launch to lay alongside. Soon after the men were on deck and the launch hoisted into place. Then, under orders, Darrin ran alongside. First of all his wounded men were passed on hoard, being there received by hospital stewards from the sick bay. Then, amid impressive silence, the two dead men were taken on board.

"Ensign Darrin," directed the officer of the deck, from the bridge, "you are directed to report to Captain Gales, at once."

Saluting, and holding himself very erect, Dave Darrin stepped proudly aboard. His face was white and angry as he neared the captain's quarters, but the young ensign strove to command himself, and tried to keep his sorely tried temper within bounds.

"You will pass inside, sir, at once," directed the marine orderly, as the young officer halted near the door.

Acknowledging the marine's salute, Dave Darrin passed him and entered the office.

Lieutenant Cantor, erect and stern, faced Captain Gales, who looked the sterner of the two.

"Ensign Darrin," began the battleship's commanding officer, rising, "most serious charges have been preferred against you, sir!"

CHAPTER X

Ensign Darrin bowed, then awaited further communication from his commanding officer.

"It was particularly set forth in the orders," resumed Captain Gales, "that any form of conflict was to be avoided by the expedition of which you commanded a part, was it not?"

"It was, sir," Darrin admitted.

"And yet, by the report which Lieutenant Cantor has turned in, you opened fire on Cosetta and his band and have returned to ship with two men killed and four men wounded. Is that report correct?"

"It is, sir," admitted the young ensign, "with one exception."

"State the exception, Ensign Darrin," ordered the captain, coldly.

"The exception, sir, is that Cosetta's fellows opened fire on us first."

Dave Darrin stood looking straight into Captain Gales's eyes.

"Ensign Darrin, did you do anything to provoke that fire?" asked the commanding officer.

"Yes, sir," Dave admitted.

"Ah!" breathed Captain Gales, while Cantor gave an almost inaudible ejaculation of triumph.

"What was it, sir, that you did to provoke Cosetta into ordering his fellows to fire?" questioned Captain Gales.

"Why, sir, I found and rescued the Americans after whom you sent me," Dave explained. "They were Cosetta's prisoners. There was not a shot fired on either side until after I had placed the released prisoners under the protection of my own men, and had started away with them. Then the Mexican bandits opened fire on us."

"Couldn't you have escaped without returning the fire?"

"We might have been able to do so, sir."

"Then why didn't you?" pressed the captain.

"Because, sir, I felt sure that we would lose most of our men if we tamely submitted, and ran, pursued by superior numbers, to our launch. Moreover, I was much afraid that some of the Americans we were trying to rescue would be hit."

"In your judgment, Ensign Darrin, there was no other course open save to return the fire?"

"That was my exact judgment of the situation, sir," replied the young ensign earnestly.

"And still is your best judgment?"

"Yes, Captain."

"Hm!" commented Captain Gales. "And yet you have returned to ship with your casualties amounting to thirty per cent of your command, and one-third of your casualties are fatalities."

"Those are the facts, sir," interposed Lieutenant Cantor. "Therefore, in the face of fighting against orders, and sustaining such losses to his own immediate command, I felt it my duty, sir, to prefer charges against Ensign Darrin."

"This is a most unfortunate affair, sir," commented Captain Gales.

Dave Darrin felt the hot blood mounting to his face. He tried to control his wrath, but could not refrain from asking a question. "Sir, do you wish me to hand my sword to you?" he said gravely, with a quick movement of his right hand toward his sword hilt.

"Not yet, at any rate," answered Captain Gales, calmly. "I wish to hear your story."

"Very good, sir," Dave returned, then plunged at once into a narrative that was stripped to the bare facts. He told everything from the landing of his men to the final escape from the lagoon under Mexican fire.

"Of course, sir, Coxswain Riley and Corporal Ross will be able to bear me out as to the facts of which they have knowledge. And I would suggest, sir," Darrin added, "that Mr. Carmody, who knows more of Cosetta than any of us, will be able to give you an excellent opinion of whether I was obliged to throw my command into the fight."

"How much of your ammunition did you bring back?" asked Captain Gales, his face betraying nothing of his inward opinion.

"All the Colt ammunition was used, sir."

"And the rifle ammunition?"

"I do not believe, sir, that any man brought back more than three or four of his cartridges. Some of the men, undoubtedly, have no ammunition left."

"It is evident, sir," hinted Lieutenant Cantor, "that Ensign Darrin did his best to bring on an engagement. And his thirty per cent casualty list——-"

"Thank you, Lieutenant," broke in Captain Gales. "The number of casualties, while unfortunate, is to be justified only by a decision as to whether it was expedient and right to engage the brigand, Cosetta."

Lieutenant Cantor's only comment was an eloquent shrug of his shoulders.

"Ensign Darrin," continued Captain Gales, "if your story is true in every detail, then it would appear to me that your action, while I regret the necessity for it, could hardly be avoided. In that case, your conduct does not appear to render you liable to censure. Until further notice you will continue in your duties. Lieutenant Cantor will, as early as possible, turn in a written report of the work of the expedition, and you, Ensign Darrin, will make a written report on your own part in the affair. You will make your report through Lieutenant Cantor, who will hand it to me with his own report. Lieutenant Cantor, in his report, will make such comment on Ensign Darrin's statements as he sees fit. You may go to your quarters, Darrin, and begin your report."

"Very good, sir," Darrin returned. Saluting, he left the office.

Out in the passage-way Dave encountered Dan, who had been waiting for him.

"What's in the wind?" asked Danny Grin, eyeing Dave anxiously.

"Cantor," Dave returned, grimly.

"Is he trying to make trouble for you because you behaved like a brave man?" Dan asked, angrily.

"That is his plan."

"The contemptible hound!" ejaculated Dan Dalzell. "Do you think he is going to succeed in putting it over on you?"

"That's more than I can predict," Darrin answered his chum. "Cantor is a bright man, and in rascality I believe him to be especially efficient."

"I'd like to call the fellow out!" muttered Dan.

"Don't think of it," Dave Darrin urged, hastily, for he knew only too well the quality of Danny Grin's temper when it was fully aroused. "A challenge would suit Cantor to the skies, for it would enable him to have my best friend kicked out of the Navy."

"I won't think of it, then," promised Ensign Dalzell, "unless that fellow tries my temper to the breaking point."

Dave went hastily to his own quarters, where he laid aside his sword and revolver, bathed and dressed himself. Then he sent a messenger in search of a typewriting machine. When that came Darrin seated himself before it. Rapidly, he put down all the essential circumstances of the night's work.

Scanning the sheets closely, Dave made two or three minor changes in his report, then signed it.

Through a messenger, Darrin inquired if Lieutenant Cantor could receive him. A reply came back that Dave might report to him at once.

"This is my report, sir," Dave announced,

Dave was about to turn on his heel and leave the room, when Lieutenant Cantor stopped him with:

"Wait a few moments, if you please, Darrin. I wish to run hastily through your report."

Declining the offer of a chair, Darrin remained standing stiffly.

As he went through the report, Cantor frowned several times. At last he laid the signed sheets down on his desk.

"Darrin," asked the division commander, "do you realize that you are out of place in the Navy?"

"I do not, sir," Dave answered, coldly.

"Well, you are," pursued Lieutenant Cantor. "With your talents you should engage in writing the most improbable kinds of romances."

"That report is true in every respect, sir," Dave frowned.

"It appears to me to be a most improbable report—-as highly improbable as any official report that I have ever seen."

"The report is true in every detail," repeated Dave, his face flushing.

Lieutenant Cantor rose from his desk, facing his angry subordinate.

"You lie!" he declared, coldly.

"You cur!" Dave Darrin hissed back, his wrath now at white heat.

Instantly he launched a blow full at Cantor's face. The lieutenant warded it off.

Within three or four seconds several blows were aimed on both sides, without landing, for both were excellent boxers.

Then Dave drove in under Cantor's guard with his left hand, while with his right fist he struck the lieutenant a blow full on the face that sent him reeling backward.

Clutching wildly, Cantor seized a chair, carrying it over with himself as he landed on the floor.

In an instant Lieutenant Cantor was on his feet, brandishing the chair aloft.

"Ensign Darrin," he cried, "you have made the error of striking a superior officer when on duty!"

CHAPTER XI

"I know it," Dave returned, huskily.

"You have committed a serious breach of discipline," blazed the lieutenant.

"I have struck down a fellow who demeaned himself by insulting his subordinate," Darrin returned, his voice now clear and steady. "Lieutenant Cantor, do you consider yourself fit to command others?"

"Never mind what I think about myself," sneered the lieutenant. "Go to your quarters!"

"In arrest?" demanded Dave Darrin, mockingly.

"No; but go to your quarters and remain there for the present. You are likely to be summoned very soon."

Saluting, Ensign Dave turned ironically on his heel, going back to his quarters.

In an instant Danny Grin came bounding in.

"There's something up, isn't there?" Ensign Dalzell asked, anxiously.

"A moment ago there was something down," retorted Dave, grimly. "It was Cantor, if any one asks you about it."

"You knocked him down?" asked Dan, eagerly.

"I did."

"Then you must have had an excellent reason."

"I did have a very fair reason," Darrin went on, "the fellow passed the lie."

"Called you a *liar?*"

"That was the purport of his insult," Dave nodded.

"I'm glad you knocked him down," Dalzell went on, fervently. "Yet I see danger ahead."

"What danger?" Dave asked, dryly.

"Cantor will report your knock-down feat to Captain Gales."

"Let him. When he hears of the provocation Captain Gales will exonerate me. Cantor will have to admit that he deliberately insulted me."

"If Cantor does admit it," muttered Danny Grin, doubtfully. "I haven't any faith in Cantor's honor."

"Why, he'll have to do it," Dave contended, proudly. "Cantor is an officer in the United States Navy. Can you picture an officer as telling a deliberate falsehood?"

"It wouldn't be extremely difficult to picture Cantor as doing anything unmanly," Dan replied, slowly.

"Oh, but he couldn't tell a falsehood," Darrin protested. "That would be impossible—-against all the traditions of the service."

"My infant," Dan retorted, "I am afraid that, some day, you will have a rude awakening."

While these events were happening Captain Gales was closely questioning John Carmody. Coxswain Riley and Corporal Ross of the marines had already been before him.

As Darrin left his division officer's quarters Cantor turned to wipe his stinging cheek, which he next examined closely in a glass. Then he turned back to his desk, smiling darkly.

Rapidly he wrote his comment on Darrin's report, signed his own report, and then leaned back, thinking hard.

"I'll do it!" he muttered, the sinister smile appearing again.

Picking up his pen, He began to write a separate report, charging Ensign David Darrin with viciously knocking him down while on duty.

This report Cantor folded carefully, tucking it away in an inner pocket of his undress blouse. Then, gathering up the other reports in one hand, he pushed aside the curtain and stepped outside.

"Hullo, Trent," he offered, in greeting, as that officer suddenly appeared.

"Cantor, I want to talk with you for a moment," urged Lieutenant Trent.

"Just now, I am on my way to the commanding officer with official reports," Cantor objected.

"But what I have to say is urgent," Trent insisted. "Can't you spare me just a moment?"

"If you'll be extremely brief," Cantor agreed, reluctantly.

"You may think I am interfering," Trent went on, "but I wish to say that I heard that fracas in your quarters, between yourself and Darrin. I happened to be passing at the moment."

Cantor gave an uneasy start. He felt a moment's fright, but hastily recovered, for he was a quick thinker.

"It was outrageous, wasn't it, Trent?" he demanded.

"I should say that it was," replied his brother officer, though he spoke mildly.

"I don't know what to make of young Darrin," Cantor continued. "First he insulted me, and then struck me."

"Knocked you down, didn't he?" asked Trent.

"Yes," nodded Cantor.

"What are you trying to do to that youngster?" asked Trent, coolly.

"What am I trying to do to him?" Cantor repeated, in seeming astonishment. "Nothing, of course, unless I'm driven to it. But Darrin insulted me, and then followed it up with a blow."

Trent fixed his brother officer with a rather contemptuous glance as he answered, stiffly.

"Cantor, there are two marines aft. Go and tell your version to the marines."

"Are you going to call me a liar, too?" demanded Cantor, his eyes blazing, as he turned a threatening face to Trent.

"Keep cool," urged Lieutenant Trent, "and you'll get out of this affair more easily than you would otherwise."

"But you spoke," argued Cantor, "as though you doubted my word. If you were outside my door at the time, then you know that I asked Darrin, 'Am I a liar?' Then he struck me at once."

"Are you going to prefer charges against Darrin for knocking you down?" demanded Lieutenant Treat.

"I am most certainly," nodded Cantor, taping his breast pocket wherein hay the report.

"Then I am obliged to tell you, Cantor," Lieutenant Trent went on, "that at the courtmartial I shall be obliged to appear as one of Darrin's witnesses. Further, I shall be obliged to testify that you said to him, 'you lie.' Then Darrin knocked you down, as any other self-respecting man must have done."

"But I didn't tell him he lied," protested Cantor, with much seeming warmth. "On the contrary, I asked him if he meant to imply that I lied."

"That may be your version, Cantor," Lieutenant Trent rejoined, "but I have just told you what my testimony will have to be."

"What's your interest in this Darrin fellow?" Cantor demanded, half-sneeringly.

"Why, in the first place," Trent answered, calmly, "I like Darrin. And I regard him as an excellent, earnest, faithful, competent young officer."

"But why should you try to shield him, and throw me down, if this matter comes before a court-martial?"

"Because I am an officer," replied Trent, stiffly, drawing himself up, "and also, I trust, a gentleman. It is both my sworn duty and my inclination to see truth prevail at all times in the service."

"But think it over, Trent," urged Lieutenant Cantor. "Now, aren't you ready to admit that you heard me ask, 'Am I a liar'?"

"I can admit nothing of the sort," Trent returned. Then, laying a hand on the arm of the other lieutenant, Trent continued:

"Cantor, all the signs point to the belief that we shall be at war with Mexico at any time now. We can't afford to have the ward-room mess torn by any court-martial charges against any officer, unless he richly deserves the prosecution. Darrin doesn't; that I know. I have no right to balk any officer who demands a courtmartial of any one on board, but it is right and proper that I should he prepared to take oath as to what I know of the merits of the matter. I must assume, and I hope rightly, that you really have an erroneous recollection of what passed before the blow was struck. Cantor, you have the reputation of being a hard master with young officers, but I know nothing affecting your good repute as an officer and a gentleman. I am ready to believe that you, yourself, have a wrong recollection of what you said, but I am very certain as to the exact form of the words that I heard passed. Good night!"

Barely returning the salutation, Cantor passed on to Captain Gales's office, to which he was promptly admitted.

The hour was late, but the commander of the "*Long Island*" was anxious to get at the whole truth of the evening's affair ashore, and so was still at his desk.

"Oh, I am glad to see you, Lieutenant Cantor," was the captain's greeting, as that officer appeared, after having sent in his compliments. "You have both reports?"

"Here they are, sir," replied the younger officer, laying them on the desk.

"Be seated, Lieutenant. I will go through these papers at once."

For some minutes there was silence in the room, save for the rustling of paper as Captain Gales turned a page.

At last he glanced up from the reading.

"I note, Lieutenant Cantor, that you are still of the opinion that the fight could have been avoided."

"That is my unalterable opinion, sir," replied the lieutenant.

"You are aware, of course, Mr. Cantor, that your report will form a part of the record that will go to the Navy Department, through the usual official channels?"

"I am well aware of that, sir."

"Have you any other papers to submit in connection with Ensign Darrin?"

For the barest instant Lieutenant Cantor hesitated.

Then he rose, as he replied:

"No other papers, sir."

"That is all, Lieutenant," nodded the captain, and returned his subordinate officer's salute.

CHAPTER XII

"The captain's compliments, sir, and will Ensign Darrin report to him immediately?"

Darrin had dressed for breakfast the morning after, but there were yet some minutes to spare before the call would come to the ward-room mess.

"My compliments to the captain, and I will report immediately," Ensign Dave replied.

Turning, he put on his sword and drew on his white gloves. Then, with a glance over himself, he left his quarters, walking briskly toward the commanding officer's quarters.

Captain Gales, at his desk, received the young ensign's salute. On the desk lay the papers in the matter of the night before.

"Ensign, I have gone over the papers in last night's affair," began the "Old Man," as a naval vessel's commander is called, when not present.

"Yes, sir?"

The captain's face was inexpressive; it was impossible to tell what was going on in his mind.

"I have given careful attention to your report, and also to that of Lieutenant Cantor. I have talked with Mr. Carmody, and have asked Coxswain Riley and Corporal Ross some questions. And so I have come to the decision——"

Here the captain paused for an instant.

How Dave Darrin's heart thumped under his ribs. The next few words would convey either censure, criticism or exoneration!

"——that Lieutenant Cantor's charges are not well sustained," continued, Captain Gales.

Dave Darrin could not repress the gleam of joy that flashed into his eyes. The memory of the men killed under his command and the present sufferings of the wounded had preyed upon him through a long, wakeful night.

But here was a veteran in the service, prepared, after hearing all possible testimony, to declare that he, Darrin, was not blamable!

"I had hoped," resumed Captain Gales, "that the affair on shore could he conducted without firing a single shot, However, Ensign Darrin, the fact has been established to my satisfaction that you did your work well; that you did not allow your men to fire a shot until you had been attacked in force. Nor did you fire upon Mexican troups or reputable natives, but upon a body of bandits —-outlaws—-who are enemies of all mankind. Not to have returned the fire, under such circumstances, would have been censurable conduct. That several times through the night you held your party's fire, and at no time fired oftener than appeared to be absolutely necessary, is established by the eye-witnesses with whom I have talked. Nor were the losses to your command higher than might have been looked for in a fight against superior numbers, such as you encountered. I have endorsed these views of mine upon Lieutenant Cantor's report and also upon your own. I can find no fault with your course of action."

"I cannot tell you, sir, how highly I appreciate your decision."

"Of course you do, Darrin!" cried Captain Gales, holding out his hand. "No young officer in the service enjoys being censured when he has used the very best judgment with which Heaven has endowed him. No man of earnest effort, likes to have his motives questioned. And I am happy to say, Ensign Darrin, that I regard you as the same faithful, hardworking officer that I considered you when you had not been more than three days aboard the '*Long Island.*' I congratulate you, Ensign, upon your skilful handling of a bad situation last night. Now, I am not going to keep you here longer, for mess call is due in two minutes, and you will want your breakfast."

With a heart full of joy and gratitude Dave hastened back to his quarters, where he laid aside his sword and gloves.

Just outside the ward-room door he encountered John Carmody, who appeared to have been waiting there purposely.

"Now, Mr. Darrin," cried the planter, holding out his hand, "I want to try to give you some idea of my gratitude for the magnificent work you did last night for my dear ones and our friends. I don't know how to begin, but——-"

"Please don't try to begin," laughed Dave. "An officer of the American Navy should never be thanked for the performance of his duty. I can't tell you how delighted I am that my efforts were successful, and that the scoundrels, who had tried to violate Mexico's sacred duty of hospitality, were roundly punished. Tell me, sir, how are the ladies this morning?"

"All of them are in excellent spirits, Mr. Darrin. I suppose you have not seen them yet. They are in full possession of the captain's quarters, and are at breakfast now."

The breakfast call sounded, and in twos and threes the officers of the "*Long*

Island," passed into the ward-room.

John Carmody was provided with a seat beside the chaplain.

"Darrin, you lucky dog!" called Lieutenant-Commander Denton, as soon as the officers were seated.

"Am I really fortunate?" Dave smiled back.

"Yes; for you were privileged to order the firing of the first shots in the Mexican war that is now close at hand. You are, or will be, historical, Darrin!"

Dave's face clouded as he replied, gravely:

"And I am also aware, sir, that I had the misfortune to lose the first men killed."

"That was regrettable," replied another officer, "but we of the Navy expect to go down some day. The two men who were killed died for the honor and credit of the service, and of the Flag, which we serve. It is the lot of all of us, Darrin. If war comes many a soldier and sailor will find an honored grave, and perhaps not a few here will lose their mess numbers. It's just the way of the service, Darrin!"

"Cantor, you were out of luck last night," observed Lieutenant Holton, who sat next to him.

"In what way?" asked Cantor, but he flushed deeply.

"You had only a boat ride, and missed the fight," replied Holton.

"Oh!" replied Cantor, and felt relieved, for he had thought that Holton referred to something else.

"Where are we heading now?" asked Dave.

"Didn't you notice the course?" inquired Dalzell.

"About westerly, isn't it?"

"Yes; we are bound for Vera Cruz," Danny Grin answered. "We shall be there in two hours. Mr. Carmody and his party have no notion of going back to their plantation at present. Instead, they'll take a steamer to New York."

Breakfast was nearly over when an orderly appeared, bringing an envelope, which he handed to Commander Bainbridge.

"Pardon me," said the executive officer to the officers on either side of him. Then he examined the paper contained in the envelope.

"Gentlemen," called Commander Bainbridge, "I have some information that I will announce to you, briefly, as soon as the meal is over."

Every eye was turned on the executive officer. After a few moments he continued:

"Yesterday, at Tampico, an officer and boatcrew of men went ashore in a launch from the 'dolplin.' The boat flew the United States Flag, and the officer and men landed to attend to the purchase of supplies. An officer of General Huerta's Federal Army arrested our officer and his men. They were released a little later, but Admiral Mayo demanded a formal apology and a salute of twenty-one guns to our insulted Flag. Some sort of apology has been made to Admiral Mayo, but it was not satisfactory, and the gun salute was refused. Admiral Mayo has sent the Mexican Federal commander at Tampico something very much like an ultimatum. Unless a satisfactory apology is made, and the gun salute is fired, the Washington government threatens to break off all diplomatic relations with Mexico and to make reprisals. That is the full extent of the news, so far as it has reached us by wireless."

"*War!*" exploded Lieutenant-Commander Eaton.

"We mustn't jump too rapidly at conclusions," Commander Bainbridge warned his hearers.

"But it *does* mean war, doesn't it?" asked Lieutenant Holton. "That chap, Huerta, will be stiff-necked about yielding a gun salute after it has been refused, and Mexican pride will back him up in it. The Mexicans hate us as only jealous people can hate. The Mexicans won't give in. On the other hand, our country has always been very stiff over any insult to the Flag. So what hope is there that war can be averted? Reprisals between nations are always taken by the employment of force, and surely any force that we employ against Mexico can end in nothing less than war."

As the officers left the table nothing was talked of among them except the news from Tampico.

The rumor spread rapidly forward. Cheering was heard from the forecastle.

"The jackies have the word," chuckled Dan Dalzell. "They're sure to be delighted over any prospect of a fight."

"If we have a real fight," sighed Darrin, his mind on the night before, "a lot of our happy jackies will be sent home in boxes to their friends."

"A small lot the jackies care about that," retorted Danny Grin. "Show me, if you can, anywhere in the world, a body of men who care less about facing death than the enlisted men in the United States Navy!"

"Of course we should have interfered in Mexico long ago," Dave went on. "Serious as the Flag incident is, there have been outrages ten-fold worse than that. I shall never be able to down the feeling that we have been, as a people, careless of our honor in not long ago stepping in to put a stop to the outrages against Americans that have been of almost daily occurrence in Mexico."

"If fighting does begin," asked Dalzell, suddenly, "where do we of the Navy come in? Shelling a few forts, possibly, and serving in the humdrum life of blockade duty."

"If we land in Mexico," Dave retorted, "there will be one stern duty that will fall to the lot of the Navy. The Army won't be ready in time for the first landing on Mexican soil. That will be the duty of the Navy. If we send a force of men ashore at Tampico, or possibly Vera Cruz, it will have to be a force of thousands of our men, for the Mexicans will resist stubbornly, and there'll be a lot of hard fighting for the Navy before Washington has the Army in shape to land. Never fear, Danny boy! We are likely to see enough active service!"

Dave soon went to the bridge to stand a trick of watch duty with Lieutenant Cantor.

For an hour no word was exchanged between the two officers. Cantor curtly transmitted orders through petty officers on the deck below. Dave kept to his own, the starboard side of the bridge, his alert eyes on his duty. There was no chance to exchange even a word on the all-absorbing topic of the incident at Tampico.

Vera Cruz, lying on a sandy stretch of land that was surrounded by marshes, was soon sighted, and the "*Long Island*" stood in toward the harbor in which the Stars and Stripes fluttered from several other American warships lying at anchor.

A messenger from the executive officer appeared on the bridge with the information that, after the ship came to anchor, Ensign Dalzell would be sent in one of the launches to convey the Carmody party ashore.

There was no chance for the rescued ones to come forward to say good-bye to Darrin on the bridge, for they went over the port side into the waiting launch.

Dalzell, however, manoeuvred the launch so that she passed along the ship's side.

A call, and exclamations in feminine voices attracted Dave's notice.

"Mr. Darrin, Mr. Darrin!" called four women at once, as they waved their handkerchiefs to him. Dave, cap in hand, returned their salute.

"Thank you again, Mr. Darrin."

"We won't say good-bye," called Mrs. Carmody, "for we shall hope to meet you and your splendid boat-crew again."

At that the jackies on the forecastle set up a tremendous cheering.

Not until Dave had gone off duty did another launch put out from the "*Long Island*." That craft bore to one of the docks two metal caskets. Brief services had been held over the remains of the sailor and the marine killed the night before, and now the bodies were to be sent home to the relatives.

After luncheon a messenger summoned Ensign Darrin to Commander Bainbridge's office.

"Ensign Darrin," said the executive officer, "here are some communications to be taken ashore to the office of the American consul. You will use number three launch, and take a seaman orderly with you."

"Aye, aye, sir."

Darrin went over the side, followed by Seaman Rogers, who had been in the landing party the night before, Both were soon ashore. Rogers, who knew where the consul's office was, acted as guide.

Crowds on the street eyed the American sailors with no very pleasant looks.

"Those Greasers are sullen, sir," said Seaman Rogers.

"I expected to find them so," Ensign Darrin answered.

They had not gone far when a man astride a winded, foam-flocked horse rode up the street.

"Do you know that man, sir?" asked Seaman Rogers, in an excited whisper.

"The bandit, Cosetta!" Dave muttered.

"The same, sir."

But Darrin turned and walked on again, for he saw that the recognition had been mutual.

Espying the young ensign, Cosetta reined in sharply before a group of Mexicans, whose glances he directed at Dave Darrin.

"There he goes, the turkey-cock, strutting young officer," cried Cosetta harshly in his own tongue. "Eye the young Gringo upstart well. You must know him again, for he is to be a marked man in the streets of Vera Cruz!"

It was a prediction full of ghastly possibilities for Ensign Dave Darrin!

CHAPTER XIII

Seaman Rogers led the way briskly to the American consulate.

"The consul is engaged, sir, with the Jefe Politico," explained a clerk at a desk in an outer office. "Will you wait, or have you papers that can be left with me?"

"Thank you; I shall he obliged to wait," Dave decided, "since I was instructed to hand the papers to the consul himself."

He took a chair at a vacant desk, picking up a late issue of a New Orleans daily paper and scanning the front page.

Seaman Rogers strolled to the entrance, watching the passing crowds of Mexicans.

"Is there any very late news from Tampico?" Darrin inquired, presently.

"Nothing later than the news received this morning," the clerk replied.

"The bare details of the dispute there over the insult to the Flag?" Darrin inquired.

"That is all, sir," the clerk replied.

So Dave turned again to the newspaper. Several things were happening in the home country that interested him.

"It was half an hour before the *Jefe Politico*, a Mexican official, corresponding somewhat to a mayor in an American city, passed through on his way out.

"You will be able to see the consul, now," suggested the clerk, so Dave rose at once, passing into the inner office, where he was pleasantly greeted.

Dave laid a sealed packet of papers on the desk before the consul.

"If you have time to wait, pardon me while I glance at the enclosures," said the consul.

Ensign Darrin took a seat near a window, while the official went rapidly through the papers submitted to him.

Some were merely communications to go forward to the United States in the consular mailbag.

Still other papers required careful consideration.

"If you will excuse me," said the consul, rising, "I will go into another room to dictate a letter that I wish to send to your captain."

Dave passed through another half hour of waiting.

"It will be some time before the papers are ready," reported the consul, on his return. "In the meantime, Mr. Darrin, I am quite at your service."

"I wonder if you have received any further news about the Tampico incident," Dave smiled, questioningly.

"Nothing further, I fancy, than was sent by wireless to all the American warships in these waters."

"Is that incident going to lead to war?" Darrin asked.

"It is hard to say," replied the consul, musingly. "But the people at home are very much worked up over it."

"They are?" asked Dave, eagerly.

"Indeed, yes! In general, the American press predicts that now nothing is so likely as United States intervention in this distracted country. Some of our American editors even declare boldly that the time has come to bring about the permanent occupation and annexation of Mexico."

"I hope our country won't go that far," Dave exclaimed, with a gesture of disgust. "I should hate to think of having to welcome the Mexicans as fellow citizens of the great republic."

"I don't believe that we need worry about it," smiled the consul. "It is only the jingo papers that are talking in that vein."

"How does Congress feel about the situation?" Dave asked.

"Why, I am glad to say that Congress appears to be in line for as strong action as the government may wish to take."

"It really looks like war, then."

"It looks as though our troops might land on the Mexican coast by way of reprisal," replied the consul. "That would bring stubborn resistance from the Mexicans, and then, as a result, intervention would surely follow. There may be men with minds bright enough to see the difference between armed intervention and war."

"I'm stupid then," Ensign Dave smiled. "I can't see any difference in the actual results. So you believe, sir, that the people of the United States are practically a unit for taking a strong hand in Mexican affairs?"

"The people of the United States have wanted just that action for at least two years," the consul answered.

"That was the way it looked to me," Dave nodded. "By the way, sir, did you hear anything about an armed encounter between a naval party and Cosetta's bandits last night?"

"Why, yes," cried the consul, "and now I remember that the landing party was sent from your ship. What can you tell me about that?"

Dave Darrin gave a brief account of the doings of the night before, though he did not mention the fact that he, himself, was in command of the landing party of rescuers.

"It was a plucky bit of work," commented the consul.

"Will that fight with Cosetta inflame the Mexican mind?" Dave asked.

"It is likely to have something of that effect upon the Mexicans," the consul replied, "though Mexico can hardly make any legal objection to the affair, for Cosetta is a notorious bandit, and bandits have no rights. The Mexican government appears to have been unable to rescue the prisoners, so the United States forces had an undoubted right to do so. Do you know anything about this fellow, Cosetta, Mr. Darrin?"

"I never heard of him before yesterday," Dave confessed.

"He is a troublesome fellow, and rather dangerous. More than once he has extorted large sums of ransom money for prisoners. He has a large following, even here in Vera Cruz, where he maintains his little force of spies and assassins. Whenever a wealthy Mexican hereabouts has had an enemy that he wanted 'removed,' he has always been able to accomplish his wish with the aid of this same fellow, Cosetta."

"Cosetta is in town to-day," Dave remarked.

"Are you sure of that?"

"I saw him here," Darrin replied, quietly.

"Then you must have been the officer in command of last night's landing party."

"I was." replied Dave Darrin, shortly.

"Then, Mr. Darrin," said the Consul, earnestly, "I am going to give you a bit of advice that I hope you won't disregard. Cosetta may feel deep resentment against you, for you thwarted his plans. Probably, too, you were the cause of laying several of his men low last night. Cosetta won't forget or forgive you. Whenever you are in time streets of Vera Cruz I would advise you to keep your eyes wide open. Cosetta might detail a couple of his worthless desperadoes to bury their knives in your back. This bandit has done such things before, nor is it at all easy to punish him, for the scoundrel has many surprisingly loyal friends in Vera Cruz. In a more strictly-governed country he would be arrested in the city streets as soon as pointed out, but in Mexico the bandit is likely to be a popular hero, and certainly Cosetta is that in Vera Cruz. If he were wanted here for a crime, there are hundreds of citizens who would gladly hide him in their homes. On any day in the week Cosetta could easily recruit a hundred men for his band. Perhaps he is now in town on that errand."

"I have an idea that the fellow is dangerous," Darrin nodded. "Still, here in Vera Cruz, with scores of American sailors usually in sight on the streets, it seems to me hardly likely that Cosetta would instruct his men to attack me. The sailors would interfere. Certainly they would lay hold of the assassin."

"Ah, but the sailors do not come ashore armed," the consul warned his visitor. "On the other hand, most of the Mexicans go about to-day with arms concealed about them. A fight between a sailor and a Mexican might, just now, be enough to start a riot."

Dave listened attentively. He was not in the least alarmed by the possibility of an attack being made upon his person, but he had the natural distaste of a naval officer for being the innocent cause of strained relations between his country and another nation.

When the stenographer brought in the papers that had been dictated to him, the consul looked them through, then signed them.

"Here is a packet of communications for your captain," said the consul, handing a bulky envelope to Darrin. "One of the communications enclosed, Mr. Darrin, is of so important a nature that you will have an added reason for keeping your weather eye open against any form of trouble that Senor Cosetta might start for you in the streets."

"At any time and in any place," Dave smiled, earnestly, "I would take the best possible care of official papers entrusted to me."

"I am aware of that, Mr. Darrin," replied the consul smiling. "But the paper in question is one that it would greatly embarrass the United States to have fall into improper hands. That is my only excuse for having cautioned you so particularly."

Seaman Rogers was waiting at the door. He saluted when Ensign Darrin appeared, then fell in a few paces behind his officer.

A short distance away a carriage stood before the door of a private banker. A woman of perhaps thirty came out through the doorway, carrying a small handbag.

Seeming almost to rise from the ground, so suddenly did he appear, a ragged Mexican bumped violently against the woman.

There was a scream, and in a twinkling the ragged Mexican was in full flight, carrying the handbag as he ran.

"After that rascal, Rogers!" cried Dave Darrin, aghast at the boldness of this daylight robbery.

"Aye, aye, sir, and with a hearty good will!" called back Rogers, as both sailors started in full chase.

CHAPTER XIV

A "FIND" OF A BAD KIND

In the nature of timings it could not be a long chase, for Ensign Dave Darrin was a swift runner, of many years' training.

Rogers, slim and lithe, was also an excellent runner.

Less than a block's distance, and Darrin had gripped the fleeing Mexican by the collar.

His left hand reached for the bag, and in a moment Dave had it in his custody. Not a man of the Vera Cruz police force was in sight, to whom to turn the wretch over, so Darrin flung the fellow from him.

That the handbag had not been opened Darrin was sure, for he had kept his eye upon it through the chase.

Going to the ground in a heap, the Mexican thief was upon his feet instantly. A knife glittered in his right hand as he rushed at the young ensign.

But Seaman Rogers was too quick for the fellow. One of his feet shot up, the kick landing on the Mexican's wrist. That kick broke the fellow's wrist and sent the knife spinning through the air.

"We must go back to the woman from whom this was taken," Dave declared, and he and Rogers faced about, walking briskly back to the carriage.

The woman was completely unnerved, and trembling with fright. Her coachman stood beside her, and already a crowd of a dozen curious natives had gathered.

"Is this your property, madam?" Dave Darrin inquired, holding up the bag.

"Yes, it is!" she cried, in excellent English. "Oh, thank you! Thank you!"

Hastily she opened the bag, disclosing a thick roll of bills.

"It is all I have in the world," she murmured, her eyes now filling with tears.

"It looks to me like a whole lot and then plenty more," uttered Seaman Rogers under his breath. "Whee! There must be a fortune there."

"I am afraid you will not be safe in the streets of Vera Cruz with so much money in your possession," Dave assured her gravely.

"I am going only as far as the docks," the woman answered. "If

I may have escort that far——-"

"You shall," Dave offered.

Another score of natives had hastened to the spot, and were looking on curiously with sullen, lowering faces. Darrin began to fear that the plot to rob this woman of her money was a well planned one, with many thieves interested in it.

Through the crack of a slightly opened doorway the face of Cosetta, the bandit, appeared, his evil eyes glittering strangely.

Dave looked up swiftly, his eyes turned straight on those of the bandit.

"It's a plot, sure enough!" gasped the young ensign to himself.
"We shall be attacked, and the crowd is too big for us to handle"

He was not afraid for himself, and he knew well that Seaman Rogers was "aching" for a chance to turn his hard fists loose on this rascally lot of Mexicans. But a rush would probably secure the bag of money for the bandits, and the woman herself might be roughly handled, It was a ticklish situation.

"You are from an American warship, are you not?" inquired the woman.

"From the *Long Island*, madam," the young officer informed her.

"I am an American citizen, too," she claimed.

"No matter to what nationality you belonged, we would protect you to the best of our ability," Darrin added, raising his cap.

Whump! whump! whump! whump! It was the sound of steadily marching feet. Then around the corner came a boatswain's mate and eight keep even a crowd of rascals in order men from one of the American warships. It was a shore duty party returning to a ship!

"Boatswain's mate!" Dave shouted. "Here!"

"Aye, aye, sir!"

On the double quick came the shore duty party. Dave Darrin found himself surrounded by blue jackets.

"This lady is very nervous, and with good reason," Dave explained to the boatswain's mate. "She just had a handbag of money snatched from her by a thief. The bag has been returned, and now she wishes our escort to the dock, that she may not be attacked again. She is on her way to board a ship that will take her back to the United States. Boatswain's mate, I wish you would ride in the carriage at her side, while the rest of us walk on the sidewalk close to the carriage."

"Aye, aye, sir!" responded the mate, saluting, then turning and lifting his cap gracefully to the woman. He helped her into the carriage, then took his seat beside her.

Dave and the nine seamen remained on the sidewalk, but kept close to the carriage as the horses moved along at a walk. Darrin had no further fear that another attempt would be made to seize the money by force. Eleven men from the American Navy are guard enough to keep even a crowd of rascals in order.

"Since Cosetta was looking on from the doorway, that must have been one of his jobs, engineered by him, and carried out by his own men," Dave told himself, swiftly. "Most of the men in the crowd must have been his own men, too, posted to take the money again, under pretense that a fight with sailors had started. So I've been the means of blocking another profitable enterprise for that fellow, Cosetta. By and by the scoundrel will feel a deep liking for me!"

The first thief, he whose wrist Seaman Rogers had broken, had promptly vanished. Unmolested, the blue-jackets escorted the carriage out on to a dock next to the one at which the launch from the "*Long Island*" lay.

Dave himself assisted the woman to alight from her carriage on the dock, at the end of which lay an American steamship.

After she had thanked the young officer earnestly, Darrin, cap in hand, remarked:

"I am afraid I shall have to trouble you, madam, for your name. I shall have to turn in a report on this occurrence on my return to my ship."

"I am Mrs. Alice Black," replied the woman. "My home is in Elberon, Ohio, and I shall probably go there soon after I reach New York. This steamship does not sail immediately, but my money will be safe on board with the purser."

Darrin gave his own name.

"You have done me the greatest service possible, Mr. Darrin, for you have saved me from utter poverty."

"Then I am very glad indeed," Dave assured her, and promptly took his leave.

Before going off the dock Darrin secured the name of the boatswain's mate, also, for inclusion in his report.

Then, with Rogers, he returned to the launch and was speedily back on his own ship.

The packet of papers entrusted to him by the consul were at once handed over to Captain Gales.

The launch was left fast to a swinging boom, and soon after was employed to take ashore Lieutenant Cantor, who had received shore leave for a few hours.

For the first time in several days, Dave and Dan had time to chat together that afternoon. That was after Darrin had turned in a brief report on the assistance rendered an American woman ashore.

"Cantor seems to have let up on you, apart from being as grouchy as he knows how to be," Danny Grin observed.

"That is because there is nothing he can really do to me," Dave answered, with a smile.

"Just the same," urged Dan, "I would advise you at all times to keep your weather eye turned toward that chap."

"He really isn't worth the trouble," Dave yawned, behind his hand. "And, fortunately, I shall not always be compelled to serve under him. Officers are frequently transferred, you know."

"If Cantor found the chance, you might last only long enough to be transferred back to civil life," Dan warned him. "Dave, I wish you would really be more on your guard against the only enemy, so far as I know, that you have."

"I'm not interested in Cantor," retorted Dave. "It would do me a heap more good to know what reply General Huerta will finally make to the American demand for satisfaction over the Tampico incident."

"Huerta won't give in," Dan predicted. "If he did, he would he killed by his own Mexican rabble."

"If Huerta resists, then he'll have to fight," Dave exclaimed, warmly.

"And if he fights most of the Mexicans will probably stand by him," Dalzell contended. His only hope of saving his own skin lies in provoking Uncle Sam into sending a spanking expedition. At the worst, Huerta, if badly beaten by our troops, can surrender to our commander, and then he'll have a chance to get out of Mexico alive. If Huerta gave in to us, he would have all the Mexican people against him, and he'd only fall into the hands of the rebels, who would take huge delight in killing him offhand. It's a queer condition, isn't it, when Huerta's only hope of coming out alive hangs on his making war against a power like the United States."

"Open for callers?" inquired Lieutenant Trent's voice, outside Dan's door.

"Come in, by all means," called Ensign Dalzell.

Lieutenant Trent entered, looking as though he were well satisfied with himself on this warm April day in the tropics.

"You look unusually jovial," Dan remarked.

"And why shouldn't I?" Trent asked. "For years the Navy has been working out every imaginable problem of attack and defense. Now, we shall have a chance to apply some of our knowledge."

"In fighting the Mexican Navy?" laughed Dave.

"Hardly that," grinned the older officer. "But at least we shall have landing-party practice, and in the face of real bullets."

"If Huerta doesn't back down," Dave suggested.

"He won't," Danny Grin insisted. "He can't—-doesn't dare."

"Do you realize what two of our greatest problems are to-day?" asked Lieutenant Trent.

"Attack on battleships by submarines and airships?" Dave inquired, quietly.

"Yes," Trent nodded.

"Huerta hasn't any submarines," Dan offered.

"We haven't heard of any," Trent replied, "Yet how can we be sure that he hasn't any submarine craft?"

"He has an airship or two, though, I believe," Dave went on.

"He is believed to have two in the hands of the Mexican Federal Army," Lieutenant Trent continued. "I have just heard that, if we send a landing party ashore on a hostile errand, on each warship an officer and a squad of men will be stationed by a searchlight all through the dark hours. That searchlight will keep the skies lighted in the effort to discover an airship."

"And we ought to be able to bring it down with a six-pounder shell," Danny Grin declared, promptly.

"There is a limit to the range of a six-pounder, or any other gun, especially when firing at high elevation," Trent retorted. "An airship can reach a height above the range of any gun that can be trained on the sky. For instance, we can't fire a shell that will go three miles up into the air, yet that is a very ordinary height at which to run a biplane. Have you heard that, a year or more ago, an English aviator flew over warships at a height greater than the gunners below could possibly have reached? And did you know that the aviator succeeded in dropping oranges down the funnels of English warships? Suppose those oranges had been bombs?"

"The warship would have been sunk," Darrin answered.

"Huerta's bird men might be able to give us a surprise like that," Trent suggested. "That may prove to be one of the new problems that we shall have to work out."

"Oh, I've worked that out already," yawned Danny Grin. "All we have to do is to equip our funnels with heavy iron caps that will not interfere with the draft of the furnaces, but will keep any oranges—-bombs, I mean—-from dropping down the funnels."

"All right then," added Lieutenant Trent. "We will consider Dalzell has solved the problem of keeping bombs out of our funnels. What is Dalzell going to do about contact bombs that might be dropped on deck or superstructure of a battleship?"

"All I can see for that," grinned Dan, "is to call loudly for the police."

"One biplane might succeed in sinking all the warships gathered at Vera Cruz," Trent continued.

"Was that the thought that made you look so happy when you came in here?" Dan asked, reproachfully. "The thought that you could scare two poor little ensigns so badly that they wouldn't be able to sleep to-night?"

"That was far from my plan," laughed Trent. "What I am really happy about is that, the way affairs are shaping, we shall soon be studying real war problems instead of theoretical ones."

"The question of uniform is bothering me more," Dave responded. "Do you realize, Trent, that we have only blue uniforms and white ones on board? If we land, to capture Vera Cruz, are our men to be tortured in heavy, hot, blue uniforms here in the tropics? Or are we to wear these white clothes and make ourselves the most perfect marks for the enemy's sharpshooters?"

"You should have more confidence in the men forward," half jeered the lieutenant. "Our jackies are taking care of that problem already. They are soaking nails and scrap iron in water, and dyeing their white uniforms yellow with iron rust."

"Say, that is an idea!" exclaimed Dan, sitting bolt upright. "I'm going to do that very thing to-night. I have one white uniform that isn't in very good shape."

"I suppose you fellows have heard the word?" inquired Lieutenant Holton, looking in.

"Not war?" asked Trent.

"No," uttered Holton, disgustedly. "Worse than that. Shore leave has been stopped for officers and men alike. And I was counting on a pleasant evening ashore to-night!"

"It won't bother me any," Dave announced. "I'd rather stay on board and sleep against the stirring times, when we won't be able to get sleep enough."

"What's the idea, anyway, in stopping shore leave?" asked Trent. "Is the admiral afraid that we'll start a row on shore?"

"I don't know," sighed Lieutenant Holton. "I only wish that I had got ashore before the order was handed out."

At that very moment Lieutenant Cantor, who had returned to ship, and had just heard the order, was standing before Captain Gales in the latter's office.

"But, sir," stammered the young officer, "It is absolutely necessary that I go ashore again to-morrow. It is vital to me, sir."

"I am sorry, Cantor," said Captain Gales, "but the admiral's orders leave me no discretion in the matter."

Captain Gales, as he spoke, turned his back in order to reach for a report book behind hum.

Ten minutes later Commander Bainbridge was summoned in hot haste to the Captain's office.

"Bainbridge," announced Captain Gales, his face stern and set, "at three o'clock a bulky envelope lay on my desk. That envelope contained the full plan of the Navy landing in Vera Cruz, in case such landing becomes necessary. All that we are to accomplish, and even the duties of the different officers and detachments from this fleet were stated in that letter. Not later than within the last half-hour that envelope has disappeared!"

Instantly Commander Bainbridge's face became grave indeed.

"Have you been out of the room, sir?" asked Bainbridge.

"Only once, and then, so the marine orderly at the door informs me, no one entered here."

"This is serious!" cried the executive officer.

"Serious?" repeated Captain Gales in a harsh tone. "I should say it was."

"Let us search the room thoroughly, sir," begged the executive officer.

Though no search could have been more thorough, the missing envelope was not found.

"Summon the officers—-all of them—-to meet me in the ward-room in five minutes!" rasped Captain Gales.

And there every officer of the "*Long Island*" reported immediately. After the doors had been closed Captain Gales announced the loss. Blank faces confronted him on all sides.

"Has any officer any information to offer that can throw the least light on thus matter?" demanded the Old Man, in a husky voice.

There was silence, broken at last by Lieutenant Cantor asking:

"May I make a suggestion, sir?"

"Certainly."

"How many officers, sir, visited your office after the time you are certain of having seen the missing envelope on your desk?"

"Five," replied Captain Gales. "Lieutenant-Commander Denton, Lieutenant-Commander Hansen, Lieutenant Holton, Lieutenant Trent and yourself."

"Were there any enlisted men in your office, sir?"

"None since before the letter came aboard," replied Captain Gales.

"Then I would beg to suggest, sir," Lieutenant Cantor continued, "that each of the five officers you have named, myself included, request that their quarters be thoroughly searched. If the missing envelope is not found in their quarters, then I would suggest that the quarters of every other officer on board be searched."

To this there was a low murmur of approval. The executive officer was instructed to take the chaplain, the surgeon and two other officers beside himself, these five to form the searching committee. In the meantime, the officers were to remain in the ward-room or on the quarterdeck.

Dave, Dan and Trent seated themselves at the mess table. Time dragged by. At last the searching committee, looking grave indeed, returned.

"Is this the envelope, sir?" asked Commander Bainbridge, holding it out.

"It is," replied Captain Gales, scanning it. "But the envelope has now no contents."

"We found only the envelope, sir," replied Commander Bainbridge, while his four helpers looked uncomfortable. "We found the envelope tucked in a berth, under the mattress, in the quarters of an officer of this ship."

"And who was the officer in whose quarters you found it?" demanded Captain Gales.

"Ensign Darrin, sir!" replied the executive officer.

CHAPTER XV

READY FOR VERA CRUZ

"Ensign Darrin"——and the Old Man's voice was more impressive than any officer present remembered ever to have heard it before——"what do you know of this matter?"

Though the shock had struck him like an actual blow, Dave Darrin steadied both himself and his voice as he replied:

"I know nothing whatever about it, sir, that is not common knowledge to everyone in this room."

"Then you did not take this envelope from my room?" demanded Captain Gales.

"I did not, sir."

"And you did not receive it from any one else?"

"I did not, sir."

"You have no knowledge of how this envelope came to be in your quarters?"

"I have not the least knowledge in the world, sir."

Captain Gales debated the matter in his own distressed mind. Dave Darrin stood there, white faced and dignified, his bearing perfect.

He looked, every inch a true-hearted young American naval officer. Yet he was resting under a terrible suspicion.

"You may go, gentlemen," announced the captain. "I ask you to see to it that no word of this matter leaks out among the men forward. Ensign Darrin, you will report to me at my office just as soon as you think I have had time to reach there before you."

Several of the officers walked hastily away. Others hung aloof, shaking their heads. Lieutenant Trent led about a dozen men who pressed around Dave Darrin, offering him their hands.

"It would take the strongest kind of proof to make me believe anything wrong in you, Darrin," declared Trent.

Others in the little group offered similar words of faith and cheer. But Dave broke away from them after expressing his gratitude. His head very erect and his shoulders squared, the young ensign walked to the captain's office.

"Darrin," began the Old Man, "if you are as innocent as I want to believe you to be in this matter, then do all in your power to help me clear your name."

"Very good, sir," Dave responded. "In the first place, sir, the important letter was in its envelope when I turned over to you the package entrusted to me by the consul."

"It was," nodded Captain Gales.

"And I have not since been in your office, sir. You know that of your own knowledge, and from what the marine orderly has been able to inform you, sir?"

"I am satisfied that you were not in thus office after you delivered the packet," replied the Old Man.

"Then I could not have taken it from your desk, sir."

"I am well satisfied of that," assented Captain Gales. "The only untoward circumstance is that the envelope was found in your quarters."

"Then, sir," Dave argued, "it is established that I could not have been the principal in the theft that was committed in your office this afternoon. That being so, the only suspicion possibly remaining against me is that I may have been an accomplice."

"No lawyer could have put that more clearly," replied Captain Gales.

"Now, sir," Dave continued, bravely, "if the important letter of instructions, or even if only the envelope had been handed me, is it likely, sir, that I would have hidden it under my mattress, when I might as readily have burned it or dropped it overboard?"

"Any clear-headed man, I admit," said the Captain, "would have destroyed the useless envelope sooner than have it found in his possession."

"The only possible use to which the otherwise useless envelope could have been put, sir, was to incriminate me. Would I have saved the envelope and by so doing taken a chance that could only ruin me? Of what service could the letter be to me, sir? I could not take it ashore, sir, for instance, to dispose of it to the Mexican officials, who probably would pay handsomely to get hold of the American naval plans. I have not asked for shore leave, sir. May I ask, sir, how many officers received shore leave, and used it, after I returned to the ship?"

"Only one, Darrin; that was Lieutenant Cantor."

Dave bit his lips; he had not intended to try to direct suspicion from himself to any other officer.

"So it might seem possible," mused Captain Gales, aloud, "that Lieutenant Cantor might have obtained the letter and turned over the envelope to you to destroy, Darrin. I am stating, mind you, only a possibility in the way of suspicion."

"Lieutenant Cantor and I are not on friendly terms," Dave answered, quickly. Then once more he bit his lip.

But the Old Man regarded him keenly, asking: "What is wrong between Cantor and yourself?"

"I spoke too quickly, sir," Dave confessed, reddening slightly. "I have no complaint to make against Lieutenant Cantor. The one statement I feel at liberty to make is that an antipathy exists between Lieutenant Cantor and I. I would suggest, further, that Lieutenant Cantor, even had he stolen the letter, could have taken it only after his return on board. So that he had no opportunity to carry it ashore, had he been scoundrel enough to wish to do so."

Captain Gales leaned back, blankly studying the bulk-head before him. Disturbing thoughts were now running in the Old Man's mind.

"Cantor was in this room," mused Captain Gales, "and it was some time afterwards that I missed the envelope. Then, too, Cantor fairly begged for more shore leave, and told me that it was vital to him to be allowed further shore leave. Still, again, in the ward-room it was Cantor who suggested that the officers' quarters be searched. Can it be that Cantor is the scoundrel? I hate to believe it. But then I hate equally to believe that Darrin could have done such a treasonable thing as to steal a copy of our landing instructions, prepared by the admiral and sent aboard through the consular office, so that the Mexicans ashore would not observe a great deal of communication between our ships."

After some moments of thought Captain Gales announced:

"Darrin, this thing is one of the most complex puzzles I have ever been called upon to solve. Your conduct and answers have been straightforward, and I am unable to believe that you had any hand in the stealing or handling of that accursed envelope."

"Thank you, sir!" Dave Darrin cried, in genuine gratitude.

"At dinner in the ward-room to-night I shall have Commander Bainbridge make announcement before all your brother officers of what I have just said," continued Captain Gales. "You may go now."

Yet, as he spoke, the captain rose and held out his hand. Dave grasped it, then saluted and turned away.

His bearing, as he went to Dalzell's quarters, was as proud as ever, though in his mind Dave Darrin knew well enough that he was still under a cloud of suspicion that would never be removed entirely from his good name unless the real culprit should be found and exposed.

"Moreover," Dave told himself, bitterly, "Cantor, if he is the one who has done this contemptible thing, may yet devise a way clever enough to convict me, or at least to condemn me in the service."

At dinner, before the first course was served, Commander Bainbridge ordered the ward-room doors closed after the attendants had passed outside. Then he stated that Captain Gales wished it understood that the finding of the telltale envelope under Ensign Darrin's mattress was the only circumstance against that officer, and that, in the captain's opinion, it was wholly likely that some one else had placed the envelope there with the intention of arousing suspicion against the officer named. It was further stated that, in time, Captain Gales hopes to reach all the facts in the mystery. The Captain wished it understood, stated the executive officer, that it would have been so stupid on Ensign Darrin's part to have hidden the envelope where it was found that there was no good reason for believing that Ensign Darrin was guilty of anything worse than having an enemy.

While this statement was being made Dave sat with his gaze riveted to the face of Lieutenant Cantor. The officer looked stolid, but his stolidity had the appearance of being assumed.

There was instant applause from some of the officers. This, being heard by sailors on duty outside, started the rumor that the officers had heard that an immediate landing was to be made in Vera Cruz or at Tampico. Thus, the jackies forward had an exciting evening talking the prospects over.

So Dave was not placed under charges, and the majority of his brother officers on the "*Long Island*" regarded the suspicion against him as being absurd. Yet Darrin knew that suspicion existed in some minds, and felt wretched in consequence.

Meantime, the news reached the fleet, as it reached newspaper readers at home, that General Huerta was becoming daily more stubborn. Then came the news that the Mexican dictator's refusal had been made final and emphatic.

"The house has passed a resolution justifying the President in employing the military and naval forces of the United States in whatever way he deems best in exacting satisfaction for the insult to the Flag at Tampico," spread through the ship on the evening of Monday, the 20th of April.

From then on no one in the American fleet doubted that war with Mexico was soon to begin. It was all right, the *"Long Island's"* officers declared, to talk about a mere peaceful landing, but no doubt existed that the landing of American sailors and marines would mean the firing of the first shots by resisting Mexicans which Would provoke war.

On the morning of the 21st of April the officers assembled in the ward-room as usual.

"Gentlemen," said Commander Bainbridge, calmly, in a moment when the Filipino mess servants were absent, "the present orders are that the American naval forces land and occupy Vera Cruz this forenoon. Orders for the details have been made and will be announced immediately after breakfast. That is all that I have to say at present."

That "all" was certainly enough. The blow for the honor of the Stars and Stripes was to be struck this forenoon. Instantly every face was aglow. Each hoped to be in the detail sent ashore. Then one young officer was heard to remark, in an undertone:

"I'll wager that all I get is a detail to commissary duty, making up the rations to be sent ashore."

Commander Bainbridge heard and smiled, but made no reply.

Soon after breakfast the work cut out for each officer was announced. Dave Darrin and Dan Dalzell were both gleeful when informed that they were to go ashore in the same detachment of blue-jackets. Lieutenant Trent was to command them.

"David, little giant," murmured Danny Grin, exultantly, "we appear to be under the right and left wings of that good men known as Fortune."

"I'm ready for duty wherever I'm put," Dave answered, seriously. "None the less, I'm delighted that I'm ordered ashore."

Lieutenant Cantor was greatly disappointed when he found that he was to remain aboard ship. Captain Gales had his own reasons for keeping that young officer away from shore.

Under cover on the *"Long Island"* all was bustle, yet without a trace of confusion. Officers and men had been so thoroughly trained in their duties that now they performed them with clock-like regularity.

It was a busy forenoon, yet no one observing the American fleet from the shore would have discovered any signs of unusual activity.

94

From the Mexican custom house, from the post-office, the cable station, and from the grim old prison-fortress, San Juan de Ulloa, the Mexican flag flew as usual.

In the streets of Vera Cruz natives and foreigners moved about as usual. Not even the Americans in Vera Cruz, except the consul, knew that this was the morning destined to become a famous date in American history.

At about eleven o'clock boats began to be launched alongside the American men-of-war. Men piled quickly over the sides. In number one launch Lieutenant Trent, Ensigns Darrin and Dalzell and forty seaman, with rifles and two machine guns, put away. Lieutenant-Commander Denton and Lieutenant Timson of the Marine Corps put off in launches numbers two and three with sixty marines and forty bluejackets. From the other warships detachments put off at the same time.

One cutter, occupied by fourteen marines, put off from one of the men-of-war and was rowed ashore at high speed. These men quickly landed at No.1 Dock.

"There they land—-they're unfurling the American Flag!" breathed Dave Darrin in his chum's ear.

Another cutter landed at another dock; then a launch rushed in alongside. It came the turn of the first launch from the "*Long Island*" to move in to berth at No.1 Dock, and Trent piled his party ashore, the launch immediately afterward being backed out and turned back to the "*Long Island*."

Within fifteen minutes a thousand marines and sailors had been landed.

"But where is the Mexican resistance?" murmured Danny Grin, impatiently. "Where is the excuse that was to be furnished us for fighting?"

That "excuse" was to come soon enough!

CHAPTER XVI

IN THE THICK OF THE SNIPING

Upon the landing of the first men, the Mexican custom house had been seized.

The seizure of the post-office and the cable station quickly followed.

Lieutenant Trent did not halt on the dock. Forming his men even while moving forward, Trent kept his command moving fast.

Dave was near the head of the little column, on the right flank.
Dan was near the rear.

For some distance Trent marched his men, hundreds of curious Mexicans parting to make way for the advance of the little detachment.

Finally Trent halted his men not far from the gray walls of the Castle of San Juan de Ulloa.

"I wonder if our job is to take that fortress?" murmured Dalzell, dryly.

"If that's our job," smiled Darrin, "we'll have fighting enough to suit even your hot young blood. But I don't believe we're cut out to take the castle. Look at the transport 'Prairie.' Her guns are but five hundred yards away, and trained on the fort. If anyone in San Juan opens on us the 'Prairie' will be able to blow the old fort clean off the map."

"What can we be waiting for?" asked Dan, fidgeting.

"I've an idea that we shall find out soon enough," Dave replied.

Dalzell glanced appealingly at Lieutenant Trent, who stepped over to say:

"I see you both want to know what we're to do. My orders are only general, and rather vague. Our work won't be cut out for us until the Mexican garrison starts something."

"But will the Mexicans start anything?" Danny wanted to know.
"So far they seem as patient as camels about fighting."

Another landing party, from the "Florida," moved up to position about a block away from Trent's small command.

"I don't mind fighting," sighed Dan, ten minutes later, "but waiting gets on my nerves."

All the time small detachments of sailors and marines were moving gradually through the lower part of Vera Cruz, moving from one point to another, and always the leading detachments went further from the water front.

At last Trent, receiving his signal from a distance, marched his men up the street, away from the fortress of San Juan de Ulloa.

Only a quarter of a mile did they march, then halted. Fully three hundred Mexicans followed them, and stood looking on curiously.

"I wonder if any one ashore knows the answer to the riddle of what we're doing," sighed Danny Grin.

"We're waiting orders, like real fighting men," Dave answered, with a smile.

"But there isn't going to be any fighting!"

"Where did you get that information?" Dave asked.

Noon came; no fighting had been started. By this time nearly every officer and man ashore believed that the Mexican general at Vera Cruz had decided not to offer resistance. If so, he had undoubtedly received his instructions from Mexico City.

More minutes dragged by. At about fifteen minutes past noon, shots rang out ahead.

"The engagement is starting," Dan exclaimed eagerly to his chum.

"The shots are so few in number, and come so irregularly, that probably only a few Mexican hotheads are shooting," Dave hinted, quietly. "Troops, going into action, don't fire in that fashion."

"I wonder of any of our men are firing back."

"All I know," smiled Darrin, "is that we are not doing any shooting."

Pss-seu! sang a stray bullet over their heads. Only that brief hiss as the deadly leaden messenger sang past.

Pss-chug! That bullet caught Dalzell's uniform cap, carrying it from his head to a distance some forty feet rearward.

"Whew! That gives some idea of the spitefulness of a bullet, doesn't it?" muttered Danny Grin, as a seaman ran for the ensign's cap and returned with it.

"It must be that I didn't get iron-rust enough on this white uniform," commented Dalzell, coolly, gazing down at the once white uniform that he had yellowed by a free application of iron rust. "My clothing must still be white enough to attract the attention of a sharpshooter so distant that I don't know where he is."

Still Trent held his command in waiting, for no orders had come to move it forward.

"The barracks are over there," said Dave, pointing. "So far as I have been able to judge, none of the bullets come from that direction."

Still the desultory firing continued. The occasional shots that rang out showed, however, that the Americans were not firing in force.

"There they go!" called Lieutenant Trent, drawing attention to the nearest barracks. From the parade ground in front, small detachments of Mexicans could be seen running toward different parts of the town.

"Are you going to fire on them?" asked Darrin.

"Not unless the Mexicans fire on us, or I receive orders to fire," the lieutenant answered. "I don't want to do anything to disarrange the admiral's plans for the day, and at present I know no more than you do of what is expected of us."

Suddenly the air became alive with the hiss of bullets.

"I see the rascals," cried Dave pointing upward. "They're on the top of that building ahead."

Trent saw the sharpshooters, too. Perhaps twenty Mexican infantrymen occupied the roof of a building a few hundred yards ahead. Some were lying flat, showing only their heads at the edge of the roof. Others were kneeling, but all were firing industriously.

"Forward, a few steps at a time," ordered the lieutenant. "Don't waste any shots, men, but pot any sharpshooter you can get on that roof, or any men who show themselves on other roofs as we advance."

"This work is a lot better than getting into boats and trying to take Castle San Juan," muttered Dalzell, as he drew his sword. All three of the officers now had their blades in their hands, for the swords would be useful if they were obliged to fight at close quarters.

Crack! crack! crack! rang out the rifles of Trent's detachment. But every shot told. Whenever any one of the three officers saw a man firing too rapidly that seaman was cautioned against wasting cartridges.

One of Trent's men was already wounded in the left hand, though he still persisted in firing.

At the first street crossing Trent shouted:

"Half of you men go down the street on that side, the rest of you over here. Ensign Dalzell, take command over there. Ensign Darrin, you will command here."

The street was swiftly emptied of blue-jackets. Hidden from the fire of the sharpshooters ahead, the sailors were out of immediate danger. But both Dan and Dave stationed a couple of good shots at either corner, in the shelter of the buildings and took pot shots at the snipers ahead.

"Darrin, pick out two of your best men, and send them to lie down in the middle of the street, facing that roof-top," Trent ordered, then shouted the order across the open street to Dalzell.

Thus, with four jackies lying flat in the middle of the street, and offering no very good targets to the roof snipers, and with two men behind each protecting corner, the Mexicans on the roof were subjected to the sharpshooting fire of the eight best shots in Trent's command.

"Darley, you stand here on the sidewalk, and watch the roof-top across the street," Dave ordered. "Hemingway, you get over on the other side and keep your eyes on the roof on this side of the street. If you see any one on a rooftop, let him have it as fast as you can fire."

Dan Dalzell, seeing that manoeuvre from across the street, stationed two roof-watchers similarly on his side.

"We'll stick to this sharpshooting stunt," Lieutenant Trent called in Darrin's ear, over the crackling of the rifles, "until we get a few of the Mexicans ahead. Then we'll rush their position and try to drive them from it. The only way——-"

That was as far as Lieutenant Trent got, for Dave, making a sudden leap at his superior, seized him by the collar, jerking him backward a few feet and landing him on his back.

"What the——-" sputtered Lieutenant Trent. That was as far as he got, for there was a crash, the sidewalk shook, and then Darrin quickly pulled his superior to his feet.

The report of Hemingway's rifle was not heard, but a tiny cloud of thin vapor curled from the muzzle of his uplifted weapon.

"I think I got one of the pair, sir!" called the sailor, gleefully.
"He threw up his hands and pitched backward out of sight."

Lieutenant Trent looked at the sidewalk astounded, for, where he had stood hay the broken pieces of a cookstove that had been hurled from the roof two stories above.

"That mass of iron fell right where I was standing," muttered Trent. "Darrin, I wondered why on earth you should jerk me back and lay me out in that unceremonious fashion. If you hadn't done it the cookstove would have crushed my bones to powder."

"It shows the temper of the kind of people we're fighting," muttered Darrin, compressing his lips tightly. "We'll soon have the whole city full trying to wipe us out!"

"We may as well rush that building ahead," muttered the lieutenant. "I'd rather have my men killed in open fighting than demolished by all the heavy hardware on these two blocks."

Raising his voice, Trent ordered:

"Cease firing! Load magazines and hold your fire. We're going to charge!"

From the sailormen a half-suppressed cheer arose. Hand-to-hand fighting was much more to their liking than tedious sharpshooting.

"Keep close to the building on either side of the street!" Lieutenant Trent ordered. "No man is to run in the middle of the road and make an unnecessary target of himself. Ensigns Darrin and Dalzell will run behind their men, to see that no man exposes himself uselessly."

"Fall in! Ready to charge. In single file—-charge!"

Heading the line on Darrin's side of the street, Trent dashed around the corner, leading his sailormen at a run.

Dalzell's men rushed into the fray at the same moment, Dave amid Dan, as ordered, bringing up the rear of the two files.

On the instant that the two lines of charging, cheering sailormen came into sight, the Mexicans on the roof-top redoubled their fire. It is difficult, however, to fire with accuracy at men who are running close to the buildings. Either the bullet falls short, or else goes wide of its mark and hits a wall behind the line. So Lieutenant Trent's men dashed down the street for a short distance, and pausing in the shelter of a building cheered jubilantly.

Now the Mexican soldiers above no longer had the advantage. Whenever one of their number showed his head over the edge of the roof he became a handy target for the jackies below.

Heavy shutters covered the windows on the ground floor of the building. The heavy wooden door was tightly locked.

"Ensign Darrin," sounded Trent's voice, "take enough men and batter that door down."

It took a combined rush to effect that. Several times Dave led his seamen against that barrier. Under repeated assaults it gave way.

"Through the house and to the roof!" shouted Trent. "We'll wind up the snipers!"

What a yell went up from two score of throats as the sailormen piled after their officers and thronged the stairs!

It was a free-for-all race to the top of the second flight of stairs. Over the skylight opening lay a wooden covering tightly secured in place.

"Come on, my hearties! Smash it!" yelled Trent, heaving his own broad shoulders against the obstruction.

After the skylight cover was smashed the Mexican soldiers would once more have the advantage. Only a man at a time could reach the roof. It ought not to be difficult for the defenders to pick off a Navy man at a time as the Americans sprang up.

At last the covering gave way.

"Pile up, all hands, as rapidly as you can come!" yelled Lieutenant Trent. "Officers first!"

"Officers first!" echoed Dave and Dan in a breath, all the military longing in their hearts leaping to the surface.

Then up they went, into the jaws of massacre!

CHAPTER XVII

MEXICANS BECOME SUDDENLY MEEK

Trent leaped to the roof. With his left arm he warded off a blow aimed at his head with the butt of a rifle.

Then his sword flashed, its point going clean through the body of the Mexican soldier who barred his way.

"Death to the Gringos! Death to the Gringos!" yelled the Mexicans.

But Trent drove back two men with his flashing sword. After him Dave heaped to the roof, his revolver barking fast and true.

Danny Grin followed, and he darted around to the other side of the skylight, turning loose his revolver.

The fire was returned briskly by the enemy, all of whom wore the uniform of the Mexican regular infantry.

In the footsteps of the officers came, swiftly, four stalwart young sailormen, and now the American force had a footing on the roof.

At first none of the Mexicans thought of asking for quarter. One of the infantrymen, retreating before Dalzell's deftly handled sword, and fighting back with his rifle butt, retreated so close to the edge of the roof that, in another instant, he had fallen to the street below, breaking his neck.

Ere the last dozen Americans had succeeded in reaching the roof the fight was over, for the few Mexicans still able to fight suddenly threw down their rifles, shouting pleadingly:

"*Piedad! piedad!*" (pity).

"Accept all surrenders!" shouted Lieutenant Trent at the top of his voice.

Four quivering, frightened Mexicans accepted this mercy, standing huddled together, their eyes eloquent with fear.

The fight had been a short, but savage one. A glance at the roof's late defenders showed, including the man lying in the street below, eight dead Mexicans, one of whom was the boyish lieutenant of infantry who had commanded this detachment. Nine more were badly wounded. The four prisoners were the only able-bodied Mexicans left on the roof.

"Pardon, but shall we have time for our prayers?" asked one of the surrendered Mexicans, approaching Lieutenant Trent.

"Time for your prayers?" Trout repeated. "Take all the time you want."

"But when do you shoot us?" persisted the fellow, humbly.

"Shoot you?" repeated Trent, in amazement, speaking rapidly in the Spanish he had acquired at Annapolis and practiced in many a South American port. Then it dawned upon this American officer that, in the fighting between Mexican regulars and rebels it had been always the custom of the victors to execute the survivors of the vanquished foe.

"My poor fellow," ejaculated Trent, "we Americans always pride ourselves on our civilization. We don't shoot prisoners of war. You will be treated humanely, and we shall exchange you with your government."

"What did that chap say?" Dalzell demanded, in an undertone, as Darrin laughed.

"The Mexican said," Dave explained, "that he hoped he wouldn't be exchanged until the war is over."

"There is a hospital detachment signaling from down the street, sir," reported a seaman from the edge of the roof.

Trent stepped quickly over to where he could get a view of the hospital party. Then he signaled to the hospital men, four in number, carrying stretchers, and commanded by a petty officer, that they were to advance.

"Any of our men need attention, sir?" asked the petty officer, as he reached the roof.

"Two of our men," Trent replied. "And nine Mexicans."

When it came their turn to have their wounds washed and bandaged with sterilized coverings, the Mexicans looked bewildered. Such treatment at the hands of an enemy was beyond their comprehension.

A room below was turned over for hospital use, and there the wounded of both sides were treated.

Still the firing continued heavily throughout the city. Trent, with his field glass constantly to his eyes, picked out the nearest roof-tops from which the Mexicans were firing. Then he assigned sharpshooters to take care of the enemy on these roofs.

"We can do some excellent work from this position," the lieutenant remarked to his two younger officers.

It was peculiar of this fight that no regular volleys of shots were exchanged.

The Mexicans, from roof-tops, from windows and other places of hiding, fired at an American uniform wherever they could see it.

The very style of combat adopted by the enemy made it necessary for the Americans, avoiding needless losses, to fight back in the same sniping way. Slowly, indeed, were these numerous detachments of Mexicans, numbering some eight hundred men in all, driven back.

Boom! boom! boom! The Mexican artillery now started into life, driving its shells toward the invaders.

"The real fight is going to begin now," uttered Dave, peering eagerly for a first glimpse of the artillery smoke.

"I hope the ships tumble down whole squares of houses!" was Danny Grin's fervent wish.

"If they start that, we're in a hot place," smiled Trent, coolly.

From the harbor came the sound of firing.

"Why, there's only one of our ships firing!" exclaimed Darrin. "The '*Prairie*' is using some of our guns!"

Presently the heavier detonations died out. So splendidly had the "*Prairie's*" gunners served their pieces that the Mexican artillerymen had been driven from their positions.

"These Mexicans will have to wait until they get out of range of the Navy's guns before they can hope to do much with their artillery," laughed Lieutenant Trent, then turned again to see what his sailormen were doing in the way of "getting" Mexican snipers from other roofs.

Every minute a few bullets, at least, hissed over the roof on which the detachment was posted.

Trent, believing that he was exposing more men than were needed, ordered twenty seamen to the floor below.

By one o'clock the firing died slowly away. Though the Mexicans had made a brave resistance, and had done some damage, they had been so utterly outclassed by better fighting men that they wearied of the unequal struggle.

"But when the enemy get heavy reinforcements from the rear," Trent predicted, as he stood looking over the city, "they'll put up a fight here in Vera Cruz that will be worth seeing!"

"I can't help wondering," mused Dave Darrin aloud, "what the rest of the day will bring forth."

"It will be the night that may bring us our real ordeal," hinted Lieutenant Trent.

CHAPTER XVIII

"Dalzell, I wish you would take four men and find the commanding officer ashore," requested Lieutenant Trent.

"Report to him our present position, as well as what we have done, and get his instructions."

Saluting, Dan signed to four sailormen to accompany him. Within an hour he had returned.

"We are going to hold what we have taken of the city, and probably shall push our lines further into the town. It is believed that after dark we shall have trouble with Mexican snipers."

"We have had some already," said the lieutenant grimly.

"We believe, sir," Dan reported, "that, after dark, there will be even more vicious sniping. The Mexicans are in an ugly mood, and will spare no effort to make us miserable for our audacity in landing armed men on their soil."

"And our orders?"

"You are directed, Lieutenant, to hold this roof until you have silenced all sniping within easy range, and then you are to fall back to the Post-office and report to the senior officer there. In the meantime you will send in a petty officer and sufficient force to accompany any of your wounded men who are badly enough hurt to require a surgeon's attention."

The squad that had accompanied Ensign Dalzell was immediately ordered to return with the wounded, after which Trent and his officers gave their whole attention to locating every Mexican sniper on every roof-top within six hundred yards of their position. So well was this done that at least a dozen Mexican sharpshooters were killed within the next hour.

For half an hour after that Trent surveyed every roof-top with his field glass. As no more shots crossed the roof on which the detachment was posted, Lieutenant Trent then concluded that his commission had been executed, and gave the order to return.

The Mexican dead and wounded were left in the building, a notice being posted on the door in order that the sanitary corps men might know where to find them. The four uninjured prisoners were now placed in the center of the detachment, and Trent marched his command back to the post-office. There the prisoners were turned over to the custody of the provost officer.

"Step inside, men, and you'll find something to eat," was the welcome news Trent gave his detachment of men.

Darrin and Dalzell were sent to a restaurant near by, where the officers were eating a welcome meal.

"Hadn't you better go first, sir?" Darrin asked.

"Simply because I am the ranking officer with this detachment?" smiled the lieutenant. "You two are younger, and therefore are probably hungrier than I am."

Dave was the first to finish his meal in the restaurant, and hurried to relieve Lieutenant Trent of the command of the detachment. Altogether there were now some two hundred men at the post-office station; these were being held in readiness to reinforce the American fighters in any part of the city where they might be needed.

Until after dark the "*Long Island's*" detachment remained there, enviously watching other detachments that marched briskly away.

As soon as dark had come down, the popping of rifles was almost continuous.

"I wish we had orders to clear the whole town of snipers," muttered Danny Grin impatiently.

"Undoubtedly that would take more men than we have ashore," Trent replied. "There would be no sense in occupying the whole city until we have driven out every hostile Mexican ahead of us. We might drive the Mexican soldiers much further, but the trouble is that hundreds of them have joined in the sport of sniping at the hated *Americanos*. If we pushed our way through the town, at once we would then have Mexican firing ahead of us and also at the rear. No fighting men behave well under such circumstances."

An hour later it became plain that Trent's detachment had some new work cut out for it, for a commissary officer now directed that the men be marched down the street to receive rations.

"We're going to have night work all right, then, and perhaps plenty of it," Darrin declared to his chum. "If we were going to remain here rations wouldn't be furnished us."

Trent was inside, personally seeing to matters, when a sentry halted a man in civilian clothes.

"A friend," replied the man in answer to the challenge.

"Advance and give your name," persisted the sentry.

"Lieutenant Cantor of the '*Long Island.*'"

At hearing that name, from one in civilian dress, Dave stepped forward.

"You've been halted by a man from your own ship, sir," nodded Darrin, on getting close enough to see that the man really was Cantor.

"Hullo," was Trent's greeting, as he stepped outside. "On duty, Cantor?"

"Not official duty," replied the other lieutenant.

"You are authorized to be ashore, of course?" continued Trent, surveying his brother officer, keenly, for, at such a time, it was strange to see a naval officer ashore in anything but uniform. "I have proper authority for being ashore," Cantor nodded.

"That is all, then," said Lieutenant Trent. "You may proceed, of course, but you are going to be halted and held up by every sentry who sees you. You would get through the town much more easily in uniform."

"I suppose so," nodded Cantor, and passed on.

Close at hand two revolver shots rang out.

"Ensign Darrin," Trent ordered, "take a man with you and investigate that firing. Locate it, if possible, and if any Mexican attempts to fire again, try to bring him in——-dead!"

"You will come with me," ordered Dave, turning to Coxswain Riley. That petty officer hastily filling his magazine, followed Darrin, who drew his own revolver.

Hardly had officer and man turned the corner when a pistol flesh came from the top of a house nearly at the next corner.

The bullet did not pass near enough for them to hear it. Plainly the shot had been fired at some one else.

"Keep close to the buildings," ordered Dave, leading the way toward the sniper. "I don't want that fellow to see us until we're right under him and ready to get him."

Noiselessly they went up the street. It would be impossible for the sniper to see them unless he bent out over the edge of the roof from which he was firing.

While they were advancing another shot was fired from the same roof. Watching the direction of the flash, Darrin was able to guess the direction of the man or men at whom the Mexican was firing.

"Some of our sharpshooters must still be posted on roofs," Dave whispered over his shoulder to Riley.

"I know one man who won't be doing much more on a roof, if I can get a sight of him for three seconds," gruffly answered Riley.

Then they stopped in front of the house in question.

"You slip across to the doorway opposite, and watch for your man," whispered Darrin. "I'll remain here and get any one who may attempt to run out of the house after you open fire."

Slipping across the street, Riley waited.

Scanning the house, from the roof of which the firing had proceeded, his drawn revolver in his hand, Dave made a quick discovery.

"Why, this is the very door from which I saw Cosetta peering out yesterday!" thought the young ensign. "I wonder if this is his home in Vera Cruz. I'll make a point of reporting this to Trent as soon as we return."

And then Dave heard a voice just inside the door say, in Spanish:

"You ought to stop that sniper on the roof. He took two shots at me as I came up the street."

"What infernal work is going on here?" Ensign Dave Darrin asked himself, hoarsely. "I how that voice. I'd know it anywhere. That's Cantor speaking, and he's in the house of the enemy!"

CHAPTER XIX

Crack! spoke a rifle across the street.

"I got him, sir!" cried the exultant voice of Riley. "But I'll make sure of him, sir!"

Crack! The Navy rifle spoke once more.

Noiselessly Darrin darted across the street.

On the roof of the house in which Dave had seen the bandit, Cosetta, the previous day, lay a man, his head and shoulders hanging over the edge.

"Speak softly," cautioned Darrin. "I don't want those men inside the house to hear you."

"He fell just like that when I fired the first shot, sir," Riley whispered. "I sent him the second bullet to make sure that he wasn't playing 'possum.'"

"And now," Dave ordered, "run down the street as noiselessly as you can go, and tell Lieutenant Trent that I wish he would come here in person, if possible, with a few men. Ask him, with my compliments to approach as noiselessly as possible, for I expect to make a surprise 'bag' here."

Riley glanced at his officer in swift astonishment, but he saw that Darrin was speaking seriously, so he saluted and departed at a run.

Shortly Riley was back.

"Lieutenant Trent is coming, sir," whispered the coxswain. "There he is, turning the corner now."

"Stand before this door, and if you hear anything inside, so much the better," Darrin murmured, then hastily moved down the street, saluting his superior officer as he met him.

"Riley told you, perhaps, he got the sniper, sir," Dave began, "but I have something even more astounding to report. I have every reason to believe that Lieutenant Cantor is in that house."

"A prisoner?" cried Trent, in an undertone.

"I have reason to believe that he isn't a prisoner," Dave went on. "The house is the same from which I saw Cosetta peer yesterday, and I have reason to think that Lieutenant Cantor and the bandit are on fairly good terms."

"Be careful what you say, Darrin," cautioned Lieutenant Trent. "In effect, you are accusing an officer of the United States Navy of treason!"

"That is the very crime of which I suspect him, sir," Dave answered, bluntly.

"Are you sure that your personal animosity has no part in that suspicion?"

"No dislike for a brother officer could induce me to charge him falsely," Dave answered simply.

"I beg your pardon, Darrin!" exclaimed Trent in sincere regret. "I shouldn't have asked you that."

"Here is the door, sir," Dave reported, in a whisper, halting and pointing.

"I heard some one talking in there in low tones," reported Riley. "I couldn't make it out, for he was talking in Spanish."

"I suspect that the voices were those of Lieutenant Cantor and Cosetta," Dave whispered.

"If they don't get away, we'll soon know," Trent whispered. "Stone and Root, I want you two to head the party that rushes the door. As soon as you get inside don't stop for anything else, but rush to the rear windows and shoot any one who attempts to escape by the rear fence. Now, men, rush that door!"

So hard and sudden was the assault that the door gave way at the first rush.

Revolver in hand, Dave Darrin was directly behind the two seamen who had been ordered to rush to the rear windows.

Just as the door yielded to the assault an excited voice in Spanish exclaimed:

"This way——quick!"

The two sailors, who had been ordered to do nothing else except guard the rear windows, saw a figure vanish through the cellar doorway. Leaving that individual to others, Stone and Boot dashed into a rear room, throwing up the window.

In the darkness a second man also rushed for the cellar doorway. But Dave Darrin's extended right hand closed on that party's collar.

"You're my prisoner," Dave hissed, throwing his man backward to the floor.

As several men rushed past them one sailor halted, throwing on the rays of a pocket electric light.

"You, Cantor, and here?" exclaimed Lieutenant Trent, aghast, as he recognized the features of his brother officer. "In mercy's name———-"

"Let me up," broke in Cantor, angrily, and Dave released him. "Ensign Darrin, I order you in arrest for attacking your superior officer."

"You won't observe that arrest, Darrin," spoke Trent, coldly. "I'll be responsible for my order to that effect. Now, then, Cantor, what explanation have you to offer for being in the house of Cosetta, the bandit?"

"I'll give no explanation here," blazed Cantor, angrily, as now on his feet, he glared at Trent and Darrin——-Dalzell was not there, for just at this instant the bolted cellar door, under his orders, was battered down, and Dan, with several sailormen at his back, darted down the stairs, by the light of a pocket lamp.

The cellar was deserted. There was no sign of the means by which the fugitive had escaped.

"Trent," said Cantor, with an effort at sternness, "you will not question me, here or now."

"I'll question you as much as I see fit, sir," Lieutenant Trent retorted, crisply. "Lieutenant Cantor, you are caught here under strange circumstances. You will explain, and satisfactorily, or——-"

"Lieutenant Trent," retorted the other, savagely, "while you and I are officers of the same rating, my commission is older than yours, and I am ranking officer here. I direct you to withdraw your men and to leave this house."

"And I tell you," retorted Lieutenant Trent, "that I am on duty here. You have not said that you are here on duty. Therefore I shall not recognize your authority."

"Trent," broke in the other savagely, "if you——-"

"I do," Lieutenant Trent retorted, stiffly. "Just that, in fact. In other words, sir, I place you in arrest! Coxswain Riley, I shall hold you responsible for this prisoner. Take two other men, if you wish, to help you guard him. If Lieutenant Cantor escapes, or attempts to escape, then you have my order to shoot him, if necessary."

"Darrin," snarled Cantor, "this is all your doing!"

"Some of it, sir," Dave admitted, cheerfully. "I heard you and another man talking in here, and I sent for Lieutenant Trent. As it happens, I know this to be the home, or the hanging-out place of Cosetta, and as I heard you talking just inside the door, I reported that fact to Lieutenant Trent."

"You will find nothing in this house, and I have not been, intentionally, in the house of a bandit, or in the house of any other questionable character," snarled Cantor, turning his back on Darrin. "And you are making a serious mistake in placing me in arrest."

"If your companion had been a proper one he would not have run away when American forces burst in here," Lieutenant Trent returned. "Both on Ensign Darrin's report, and on my own observation and suspicion, I will take the responsibility of placing you in arrest. I shall report your arrest to the commanding officer on shore, and will be guided by his instructions. You will have opportunity to state your case to him."

"And he will order my instant release as soon as he hears why I am on shore. Trent, you have made a serious mistake, and you are continuing to make it by keeping me in arrest."

"Sorry, Cantor; sorry, indeed, if I am doing you an injustice," Lieutenant Trent answered, with more feeling. "Yet under the circumstances, I cannot read my duty in any other way."

"You'll be sorry," cried Cantor, angrily.

"I don't know what to make of this, sir," Danny Grin reported, a much puzzled look showing on his face. "That cellar door was shut and bolted in our faces. We smashed the door instantly, and rushed down the stairs. When we reached the cellar we found it empty; whoever the man was he escaped in some way that is a mystery to me."

"Have you thought of the probability of a secret passage from the cellar?" inquired Trent.

"Yes, sir, and we've sounded the walls, but without any result."

"I'll go below with you," offered Trent. "Ensign Darrin, bear in mind that we are in danger of being surprised here, and would then find ourselves in something of a trap. Take ten men and go into the street, keeping close watch."

Twenty minutes later Trent came out, followed by his command, with whom marched the fuming Cantor, a prisoner.

"Darrin, there must be a secret passage from the cellar," Trent told his subordinate, "but we have been unable to find it. We are bringing with us the body of the sniper that Riley shot on the roof."

Line was formed and the detachment started back, Danny Grin and two sailormen acting as a rear guard against possible attack.

Arrived at the post-office Trent, accompanied by Cantor and the latter's guards, hurried off in search of the commanding officer of the shore force.

Fifteen minutes later Lieutenant Trent returned.

"I was sustained," he informed Dave and Dan. "It was tough, but the commanding officer directed me to send Cantor under escort back to the '*Long Island*,' with a brief report stating why that officer was placed in arrest."

There followed more waiting, during which the sound of individual firing over the city became more frequent. Cantor's guard returned from the "*Long Island*," with word that Captain Gales had ordered that officer in arrest in his own quarters.

At last orders for Trent's detachment arrived.

"We are to push on into the city," Trent informed his ensigns. "Twenty more '*Long Island*' men will reach us within three minutes. We are to silence snipers, and kill them if we catch them red-handed in firing on our forces. Above all, we are directed to be on the alert for any Americans or other foreigners who may be in need of help. We are likely to have a busy night."

Then, turning to his men, he added:

"Fall in by twos! Forward, march!"

CHAPTER XX

Trent saw his reinforcements approaching, and advanced to pick them up and add them to his command.

The column, now a strong one for patrol purposes, turned at right angles at the first corner, and marched on into the city, from the further side of which came the sound of firing.

Every man with the column carried a hundred and fifty rounds of ammunition. A machine gun was trailed along at the rear, in the event that it might be wanted.

Less than half a mile from the start, Lieutenant Trent's command sighted the American advance line ahead. Some of the seamen and marines in this advanced line occupied rooftops and kept up a variable, crackling fire.

As Trent approached the line, a lieutenant-commander approached him.

"Do you come to reinforce us, Lieutenant?" he inquired.

"No, sir," Trent answered. "We are to patrol, and to took out for Americans and other foreigners who may be in danger."

"Then I would caution you, Lieutenant, that this is the outer line. If you get ahead of us, take extreme care that you do nothing to lead us to mistake you for Mexicans."

"I shall be extremely cautious, sir," Trent replied, saluting, then marched his command through the line and on up the street.

"Good luck to you," called several of the sailors in the line. "Bring us back a few Mexicans!"

"We'd like to, all right," replied Riley, in an undertone.

"Ensign Darrin, take a petty officer and four men and lead a point," Lieutenant Trent ordered. "I don't want the 'glory' of running a command into an ambush."

Calling to Riley and four sailormen, Dave led them down the street at the double-quick until he was two hundred yards in advance Then he led his men on at marching speed.

The work at the "point" is always the post of greatest danger with a marching command. This point is small in numbers, and moves well in advance. If the enemy has posted an ambuscade on the line of march it is the point that runs into this danger.

As they marched Dave did not preserve any formation of his men. His detachment strode forward, alert and watchful, their rifles ready for instant use.

Three blocks away a horse stood tethered before a door. Hearing the sound of approaching feet a man looked hurriedly out of the doorway. Then he rushed to the horse and untied it.

"Halt!" Shouted Ensign Darrin, as he saw the man dart from the doorway. "Halt!" he ordered, a second time, as the man seized the horses's bridle ready to mount.

Quick as a flash the stranger drew a revolver, firing two shots down the street.

"Fire! Get him!" shouted Darrin.

Five rifles spoke, instantly. Just in the act of reaching the saddle the stranger plunged sideways, fell to the roadway, the startled horse galloping off without its rider.

"Don't run to him," commanded Dave Darrin. "We'll reach him soon enough."

Close at hand it was seen that the man was in the uniform of a Mexican officer. His insignia proved him to be a major.

"Dead," said Riley. "Two pills reached him, and either would have killed."

Dave nodded his head in assent, adding:

"Leave him. Our work is to keep the point moving."

When they had gone a quarter of a mile further, a sound of firing attracted the attention of the American detachment.

"Lieutenant Trent's compliments, sir," panted a breathless messenger, saluting, "and you will turn down the next corner, Ensign, and march toward the firing."

After a few minutes Dave sighted a large building ahead. He did not know the building, then, but learned afterwards that it was the Hotel Diligencia.

Almost as soon as Darrin perceived the building, snipers on its roof espied the Navy men.

Cr-r-rack! The brisk fire that rang out from the roof of the hotel was almost as regular as a volley of shots would have been.

116

Darrin ordered his men to keep close to the buildings on either side of the street, and to return the fire as rapidly as good shooting permitted.

"Drive 'em from that roof," was Darrin's order.

Lieutenant Trent arrived on the double-quick with the rest of the detachment.

"Give it to 'em, hot and heavy!" ordered Trent, and instantly sixty rifles were in action.

Suddenly a window, a some distance down the street from the Americans opened, and a man thrust a rifle out, taking aim. That rifle never barked, for Dave, with a single shot from his revolver, sent the would-be marksman reeling back.

"Watch that window, Riley, and fire if a head appears there," Dave directed. "There may be others in that room."

Cat-like in his watchfulness, Riley kept the muzzle of his weapon trained on that window.

"Look out overhead!" called Danny Grin, suddenly.

From the roofs of three houses overlooking the naval detachment fire opened instantly after the warning. Two of the "*Long Island's*" men dropped, one of them badly wounded.

Then the sailormen returned the fire. Two Mexicans dropped to the street, one shot through the head; the other wounded in the chest. Other Mexicans had been seen to stagger, and were probably hit. Thereafter a dozen seamen constantly watched the roofs close at hand, occasionally "getting" a Mexican.

"I know what I would do, if I had authority," Darrin muttered to his superior. "I'd send back for dynamite, and, whenever we were fired on from a house I'd bring it down in ruins."

It was a terrible suggestion, but being fired upon from overhead in a city makes fighting men savage.

Evidently the Mexicans on the hotel roof had been reinforced, for now the fire in that direction broke out heavier than ever.

"Shall I have the machine gun brought up, sir?" Dave hinted.

"Yes," approved Trent, crisply. "We'll see what a machine gun can do when brought to bear on a roof."

So Ensign Darrin ran back to give the order. The gun was brought up instantly, loaded, aimed and fired.

R-r-r-rip! Its volleys rang out. A rain of bullets struck at the edge of the hotel roof, driving back the snipers amid yells of pain.

Yet the instant the machine gun ceased its leaden cyclone the snipers were back at work, firing in a way that showed their rage.

"We can keep 'em down with the machine gun," declared Trent, "But it might take all the ammunition of the fleet to keep it running long enough unless we can make more hits."

In their recklessness the Mexicans exposed themselves so that four more of them fell before the seamen's rifles.

"Probably the Mexicans can get reinforcements," Dalzell muttered. "Though we may hit a few in an hour's firing, they can replace every man we hit."

"At least we can give those fellows something to think about between now and daylight," Dave returned, compressing his lips grimly.

"Grenfel is wounded, sir, and Penniman has just been killed," reported a petty officer, saluting.

Lieutenant Trent hastened back to confirm the death of Penniman, and also to see if anything could be done for the comfort of the wounded man. He decided to send Grenfel back, two sailormen being detailed for that purpose.

"Look out for snipers," the officer warned the bearers of the wounded man. "Carry your rifles slung and be ready for instant work. If we hear you firing behind us I'll send men to help you through."

Along the street, ahead of the detachment, a man came crawling from the direction of the hotel.

In an instant a dozen sailormen leveled their weapons.

"Hold up there, men!" Darrin called, sharply.

"Don't shoot at him."

An instant later snipers on the hotel roof discovered the crawling man, opening fire on him so briskly that the endangered one rose to his feet and came sprinting toward the sailors with both hands uplifted.

"Lower your hands!" shouted Darrin. "They make targets. We won't fire on you!"

That the man understood English was plain from his instant obedience. With Mexican bullets raining about him, the fugitive came on at headlong speed.

"Here! Stop!" Ensign Darrin ordered, catching the man and swinging him into a doorway. "Keep in there, and you're safe from the enemy's fire."

Swiftly Lieutenant Trent crossed the street to hear the escaped one, whom Darrin was already questioning.

"You're an American?" asked Dave.

"Yes!" came the answer.

"How did you come to be here?"

"Escaped from the basement of the hotel. I knew it was up to me to get through to you if I could live through the storm of bullets that I knew would be sent after me. My news is of the utmost importance!"

Then, to the astounded American Navy officers the stranger made this blood-stirring announcement:

"In the Hotel Diligencia are at least twenty American women!"

CHAPTER XXI

"You're sure of that?" breathed Trent, tensely.

I ought to be, uttered the man, hoarsely. "One of the women is my wife, and another is my daughter! I haven't seen any of the women in five hours."

"How so?" asked Trent, sharply.

"The soldiers thrust me into the basement. Ever since I found myself alone I've been working with a penknife to dig out the mortar of the bricks in which the window bars were imbedded."

"The instant I had jerked enough bars loose I crawled through the opening and started for you."

Giving swift instructions to keep the machine gun going continuously, and to keep the fire trained on the edge of the hotel roof, Trent detailed four riflemen to remain with the machine gun man, then led the rest swiftly under the hail of bullets that raged over their heads.

In this mode of attack the sailormen gained the sidewalk under the hotel without a shot having been fired from the roof.

"Ensign Darrin, lead as many men as you can against the doors!" ordered the lieutenant. "Get them down as fast as you can!"

Their first assaults against the massive doors failing, four sailors were sent on a run for some form of battering ram. They returned with half of a telegraph pole that had been cut in two by shell fire in the afternoon.

Borne by a dozen stout jackies, the pole was dashed against the door. At the second assault the lock was broken. Dave dashed into the hotel at the head of his squad.

"Straight to the roof, Ensign Darrin!" shouted Lieutenant Trent. "Ensign Dalzell, you will take ten men and endeavor to find the American women."

Then Trent, with the remainder of the command, rushed on after the advance guard. Up the stairs dashed Dave in the lead. The skylight proved not to be fastened.

Only a minute before had the machine gun stopped its murderous hail. Now some thirty Mexican soldiers crept to the edge of the roof to try their luck again with the sailormen up the street.

"There is only a handful of them," shouted one Mexican. "The gringos must be under the hotel, or in it!"

At that announcement there was a swift rush toward the skylight. Just before they reached it Darrin sprang into sight, followed by his men. Short, sharp conflict followed. Twelve Mexicans, three of them killed, went down, and two American sailormen had been wounded when the enemy sent up their appeal for "*piedad*," or quarter.

Saluting, a sailorman reported to Lieutenant Trent that Ensign Dalzell had found the American women in the annex of the hotel. None had been injured, but all were much frightened.

Leaving a petty officer in charge on the roof, Trent turned to Dave to say:

"Come along, Darrin. We'll see what can be done for our countrywomen."

Hastily descending, and following the messenger, the two officers were met at the door of a spacious room by Ensign Dalzell.

"Ladies," said Dan, turning, "here are Lieutenant Trent and Ensign Darrin. The former commands this detachment."

On the floor lay more than a dozen wounded Mexicans.

Two of the American women, having had nursing experience, had taken good care of the injured.

"Ladies," asked Lieutenant Trent, "have you been roughly treated by the Mexicans?"

"Far from it," said one of the women. "The Mexican officer in command treated us with great consideration. We were in the main part of the hotel, the wooden building. The Mexican officer told us that his men were going to occupy the roof as a military necessity, and that there would be fighting. He assured us that we would be safer in the annex, and escorted us here."

"Where is that officer now?" asked Trent, promptly. "I would like to shake hands with him."

"I am afraid you would have to travel inside the Mexican lines," said another woman. "A little while ago a party of horsemen rode up to the rear of the hotel, and one officer, a lieutenant-colonel, came up into the hotel and sought the officer in command here, ordering him to withdraw with his men, leaving only a few behind to keep up a show of resistance."

"I will see that you are taken at once inside the American lines," declared

Trout. "There you will be safe."

Preparations were quickly made. The Mexican prisoners who were able to walk were formed under guard. The American women walked on ahead of the prisoners. Ensign Darrin, with half of the command, took charge of the rescued women and prisoners, and went to the lower part of the town, to turn over the refugees and prisoners.

Trent posted a squad of his men, under Boatswain's Mate Pearson, on the roof. The rest of the seamen were stationed in the street, and Dave was placed in immediate command, with instructions to keep a sharp lookout on all sides. The boatswain's mate was to report to him anything observed from the roof.

In half an hour Danny Grin's detachment returned, coming almost on the double-quick. Dalzell, wide-eyed with news, drew his brother officers aside.

"Cantor has escaped!" Dan murmured, excitedly. "It was not widely known on the 'Long Island' that he was in arrest. So it seems that he went down over the side, stepped into a gig, and ordered the coxswain to take him ashore. As he was in civilian dress he was not likely to be closely observed by sentries on shore, and so far no trace of him has been discovered."

"I believe he has left the Navy," Dave nodded. "Further, as he appeared to have strange interests ashore, I believe that he has deserted to the enemy."

"Don't say that," begged Trent earnestly. "Bad as he may have been, Cantor was trained in all the traditions of the Navy. I can believe him wild, or even bad, but I can't believe him big enough scoundrel to desert to the enemy."

"It's a fearful thing to believe," Darrin admitted, "but what are we to believe? We found him in the house of that notorious bandit, Cosetta. Do you feel any doubt, sir, that Cosetta has proposed, or will propose to the Huerta government that he bring his men in under the Mexican flag in return for a pardon? There is another side to it, sir. The landing plans were stolen from Captain Gales's desk. Doesn't it now seem likely that Cantor stole the plans, and turned them over to Cosetta, who would be delighted at the chance of being able to turn them over to the commander of the Mexican forces around Vera Cruz?"

"The suspicion seems plausible enough," Trent admitted, sadly, "yet it is a terrible thing to believe."

"What's that?" cried Dan, jumping suddenly as shots rang out in another street close at hand.

First had come three or four shots, almost immediately a crashing fire had followed.

"Ensign Darrin," ordered Trent, promptly, "take thirty men and locate that firing. If you run into anything that you cannot handle, rush word back to me."

Like a shot, Dave Darrin was off, running at the head of thirty sailormen. Around two corners they dashed, then came in sight of a scene that made their blood boil.

Some forty men stood in the street, firing at a house from whose windows flashes of pistol shots came. Plainly the defenders were pitifully weak. Up to this moment the men in the street had not observed Ensign Dave's party.

"Sprint down close enough, Riley," Dave directed, "to see whether the men in the street are Mexicans or our own men. I suspect they're Mexicans."

"They're Mexicans, sir!" panted Riley, returning at a sprint.

"Ready! Aim! Fire!" shouted Darrin. "Charge. Fire as you need."

As the volley rang out several Mexicans dropped. Dave dashed down the street at the head of his men.

A feeble return of the fire came from the Mexicans, who then broke and fled to the next corner.

"Are there Americans inside the house?" called Dave, halting before the open but darkened windows.

"Indeed there are!" came a jubilant voice. "Are you Americans?"

"From the '*Long Island*,'" Dave answered. "Come out and join us, and we'll take you to safety."

"Now, heaven be praised for this!" answered the same man's voice, devoutly. "Come, my dear ones. We are under the protection of our own Navy men."

Out into the street came a man and woman past middle age. Behind them followed a man of perhaps twenty-five, and a woman who was still younger.

"I am Ensign Darrin, at your service," Darrin announced, raising his cap.

"We were never so glad before to see a naval officer, Mr. Darrin," responded the older man, heartily. "Tom and I had only our revolvers with which to defend ourselves. Permit me. I am Jason Denman. This is my wife, this our daughter, and this our son."

Dave stepped closer to acknowledge the introduction. When, in the darkness, his gaze rested on the young woman, Ensign Darrin gave a gasp of surprise.

"You are wondering if we have met before," smiled the young woman, sadly. "Yes, Mr. Darrin, we have. You thrashed that bully, Mr. Cantor, one night in

New York."

"I did not know, then, that he was a brother officer," murmured Dave, "but I would have struck him even if I had known."

"He was here to-night, with the Mexicans whom you drove away," continued the young woman.

"With Mexican soldiers?" gasped Darrin.

"There were but a few soldiers," Miss Denman continued. "The rest were Mexican civilians, brigands, I believe."

"Before I can discuss matters," Darrin replied quickly, "I must get you to a place of safety. You will please march in the middle of this small command. Fall in, men, by fours."

As quickly as possible the line was in motion. Dave marched back to the Hotel Diligencia, where he made instant report to his superior.

"This is the worst news possible!" gasped Lieutenant Trent. "I must send word to the commanding officer downtown, and will do so by Dalzell, who will take thirty men and escort the Denmans to safety."

"As to Lieutenant Cantor, sir," Dave asked his commander. "He is to be arrested wherever found, I suppose?"

"He is to be arrested," replied Trent, between closed teeth. "If be resists arrest, or if he fires upon our party, he is to be shot at once."

"Shot?" gasped Dave Darrin.

"You have your orders, Darrin, and they are proper, legal orders."

"And I shall obey the order, if need arise."

From across the street, as Darrin finished speaking, a window was raised and several rifles were aimed directly at him. Then shots rang out.

CHAPTER XXII

Unconsciously Ensign Dave Darrin swayed slightly, so close did the shower of bullets pass him.

Then the reports of more than a score of American rifles rang out just as Danny Grin reached his chum's side.

"Hurt, David, little giant?" asked Dan.

"Not even touched, so far as I know," smiled Darrin.

"Boatswain's mate, take a dozen men and leap into that house through the open window!" Lieutenant Trent called, sternly.

Then the senior officer hurried over to the subordinate.

"Did the rascals get you, Darrin?" demanded the lieutenant, anxiously.

"I don't think so, sir," was the reply. "I don't believe I've a scratch."

"It's a marvel," gasped Trent, after having taken a pocket electric light and by its rays examined the young ensign. "I believe every one of those Mexicans aimed at you."

"It seemed so, sir," Dave laughed.

Danny Grin had already gone, and without orders. The instant he was satisfied that his chum was uninjured Dalzell had leaped away in the wake of the party led by the boatswain's mate. Now Dan was climbing in through the window, helped by two seamen who had been left on guard outside.

But the search of the house revealed only one dead Mexican, not in uniform, who had been killed by the sailormen's fire, and a trail of blood that must have been shed by the wounded enemy as they were carried away.

"Bandits—-Cosetta's men—-not soldiers, this time," was Dan's instant guess.

The miscreants and their wounded, as the blood trail showed, had escaped by way of the rear of the house. None were in sight by the time the Americans reached the back yard.

"Shall we pursue, sir?" asked the boatswain's mate, saluting.

"In what direction?" asked Dalzell, scanning the ground. "The rascals can run faster than we can follow a trail of blood. But you may go back to Lieutenant Trent, report just what we have found, and bring me his orders."

"Lieutenant Trent believes that you are not likely to catch up with the fugitives, and there would be danger of running a handful of men into a cunning Mexican ambush," the petty officer reported, two minutes later.

After that the night dragged slowly. Trent allowed some of his men to sleep in doorways an hour or so at a time, but there were enough sailormen awake to handle any sudden surprise or attack.

At four in the morning Trent's command was relieved by a company of marines with two machine guns.

Lieutenant Trent, under orders, marched his command back to a park in which tents had been pitched. Here, under blankets on the ground, the tired sailormen and their three officers were allowed to sleep until noon.

By daylight of that day, Wednesday, the first detachment ashore had been strongly reinforced.

There was still much sniping in the city, though now the firing came mostly from the rear of the town. Slowly, patiently, the Navy detachments pushed their way forward, attending to snipers and also searching houses for concealed arms and ammunition.

In the course of this search hundreds of Mexicans were arrested. Even some very small boys were found with knives.

On the third day the residents of the city were warned that all who possessed arms must take their weapons to the provost officer's headquarters. About nineteen hundred men, women and boys turned in their weapons, running all the way from the latest models of rifles down to century-old muskets.

Soon after orders were issued that all natives found armed were to be executed on the spot. To the average American this might have seemed like a cruel order, but now the list of dead sailormen and marines had reached twenty-five, and there were scores of wounded American fighting men. Stern steps were necessary to stop the deadly sniping.

Another day passed, and Vera Cruz, now completely occupied by the Americans, had ceased to be a battle ground. Now and then a solitary shot was heard, but in every instance the sniper was tracked down, and his fate provided another tenant for the Vera Cruz burying ground.

Detachments were now posted even to the suburbs of the city.

On the morning of the fifth day, just after Trent's detachment had been roused from a night's sleep in a park in the heart of Vera Cruz, orders came to the lieutenant that seemed to please him.

"We are to march as soon as we have had breakfast," Trent told his two junior officers. "We are to take position a mile and a half south-west of the advanced line, and there wait to protect, if necessary, the Navy aviators, who are going out soon on a scouting flight. At the same time, we are to keep a lookout for the appearance of one of the airships that the Huerta forces are supposed to possess. If we see one, we are to try to get it with the machine guns or rifles. And here is a piece of news that may interest you youngsters. If requested by either of the Navy aviators, I am to allow one of my junior officers to go up in the airship to help with the preparation of field notes to be used in making a military map. If such a demand be made upon me, which of you young men shall be the one to go?"

Ensigns Dave and Dan had turned glowing faces to Trent. Then they glanced at each other. A scouting trip in one of the Navy aircraft would be an unqualified delight to either.

"Let Darrin go," urged Danny Grin.

"I withdraw, in favor of Dalzell," spoke Dave, with equal quickness.

"Which shall it be, then?" Trent demanded quizzically.

"Dalzell," said Dave.

"Darrin," decreed Danny Grin.

"How am I to decide?" asked the lieutenant, smiling at the two eager faces. Then, suddenly he added: "I have it! Which excelled the other in map work at Annapolis?"

"Darrin had the higher marks! I defy you to dispute that, David, little giant."

As Danny Grin's statement was true, Dave could not dispute it, so be contented himself by saying:

"Dalzell's map-work at Annapolis was good enough to suit any need around here, and I shall be glad to see Dalzell get the chance."

"On that showing," returned Trent, "Darrin shall have the chance if it comes this way."

After a quick meal the detachment was under way. In about an hour the position ordered had been taken.

"Here comes the first Navy birdman!" cried Dan suddenly, pointing townward.

Just appearing over the housetops, and soaring to an elevation of a thousand feet, came one of the huge hydro-aeroplanes in which Navy aviators had long been practicing for just such work as this. Capable of coming down and resting on the water, or of rising from the same, these aircraft were ideally suited to the work. Swiftly over Vera Cruz came the airship, then straight out over the advanced line, and next on toward the detachment beyond.

"He isn't coming down," cried Danny Grin in a tone of genuine disappointment. "No chance for you on that one, Davy! Too bad!"

Yet suddenly the rattling noise nearly overhead almost ceased as the engine was shut off. Then gracefully the craft voloplaned and touched the ground, just inside the detachment's line.

"Great work, Bowers!" cried Trent, recognizing in the Navy birdman a former classmate at Annapolis.

"Thank you, Trent. You have an officer, haven't you, to help me with field notes on this survey?"

"I have two," smiled Trent, "but I am afraid I can spare only one. Lieutenant Bowers, Ensign Darrin. Hop aboard, Darrin!"

In a twinkling Ensign Dave had shaken hands with the birdman, adding:

"At your orders, sir!"

Then Dave stepped nimbly up to the platform. "Take a seat beside me, with your field-glasses ready. Here's your field note-book."

At a sign from Lieutenant Bowers, the eager sailormen parted in front of the airship, which, after a brief run, soared gracefully once more.

Behind Lieutenant Bowers stood a sailor with a signal flag.

"Step to the rear," Bowers directed, over his shoulder, "and wigwag back: 'O.K. Stopped only for assistant.' Sign, 'Bowers.'"

"Aye, aye, sir," answered the signalman. "Lieutenant Sherman's airship is rising from the harbor, sir," reported the signalman.

"Very good," nodded Lieutenant Bowers, and kept his eyes on his course. "Darrin, are you taking all the observations necessary and entering them?"

"Aye, aye, sir."

"There's the railroad bridge about which the admiral was so anxious," said Bowers, presently. "You will note that the bridge stands, but the railroad tracks have been torn up."

"Aye, aye, sir," Dave reported, after using his field glass.

"That's one of the things we wanted to know," Bowers continued. "And keep an especially sharp lookout, Ensign, for any signs of Mexican forces, hidden or in the open."

But, though Dare looked constantly, he saw no indications of the Mexican column with which General Maas had retreated.

"Too bad about Cantor of your ship," murmured Lieutenant Bowers, a little later. "Though the forces have been searching for him for three or four days he can't be found anywhere. It must be fearful to be tried for treason to one's flag. I am hoping that Cantor will be brought in dead. Under such charges as he faces, there's more dignity in being dead."

"Much more," Dave assented, in a low voice.

On and on they flew. Once, when Dave sighted moving persons in the distance, Bowers drove the craft up to three thousand feet above the earth. But soon, under the glass, these suspects turned out to be a party of wretched refugees, hurrying, ragged, barefooted, starving, gaunt and cactus-torn, to safety within the American lines at Vera Cruz.

For many miles Bowers's craft flew inland, and much valuable information was picked up, besides the data from which any naval draughtsman could construct a very good map of that part of the country.

At last Lieutenant Bowers turned back.

Suddenly Dave exclaimed, "Hullo! There are two men coming out of the adobe house ahead."

The house in question was out about four miles beyond Trent's station.

Dave kept his glass turned on the two men on the ground, at the same the trying to conceal the glass from their view.

"They haven't rifles," he told Lieutenant Bowers. Then, as the aircraft passed and left the adobe house to the rear, Darrin bent over and whispered something in Bowers's ear that the signalman behind them could not hear.

CHAPTER XXIII

THE DASH FOR THE TRAITOR

A Little later the hydro-aeroplane returned to Lieutenant Trent's position.

Dave placed in the hands of the lieutenant the field note-book, which had been so carefully kept that any officer could draw a map from it at need.

Lightly the big airship touched the earth just inside Trent's line. Dave, shaking hands with his temporary commanding officer, added:

"Thank you for something I've always wanted—-a flight over a real enemy's country."

"I've greatly enjoyed having you with me," Lieutenant Bowers responded. "Trent, you've obliged me hugely by giving me so good an assistant. Good-bye, fellows."

The birdman was again several hundred feet up in the air.

"What kind of a trip was it?" asked Dalzell.

"It was wonderful," Dave breathed. "And I've brought back news of great importance!"

"Did you get it from Mexico City or Washington?" Trent broke in.

"Of course not," Dave said, wonderingly.

"Then you've no such news as we can tell you," Danny went on, quickly, sadly. "Can you guess what it is?"

"Our government isn't going to surrender us to the Huerta forces, is it?"

"Not quite so bad as that," Dan admitted. "But listen! The governments of Brazil, Argentine and Chili have offered their services in arranging mediation between Washington and Mexico City. And Washington has accepted!"

"No war?" gasped Dave Darrin, thunderstruck. "No war against a country that has treated our citizens so outrageously? Has Huerta accepted, too?"

"We haven't heard, as yet," Trent took up the thread of information, "but there is a rumor that Huerta will be only too glad to accept, even if only as a bluff. If, by any kind of a scheme, he can hold us off for a few weeks, he will then have his army consolidated, will have the railroad and bridges destroyed, and the mountain roads to Mexico City all planted with mines, and then be able, most likely, to make the advance of our Army to Mexico City cost us hundreds of good Yankee lives per mile!"

"And Funston's brigade of regulars is on the way, too!" Danny Grin added, sorrowfully. "Won't there be some mad soldier-boys?"

Ensign Dave Darrin stood with bowed head for a few moments. To him it seemed hard indeed, if the Mexicans, after almost countless outrages against American citizens, even to the extent of assassination——-and worse——-were to escape their richly deserved punishment through a few tricks of diplomacy.

Then the spirit of the service, so strong in him, came to the surface. To others belonged the right of command, his only the privilege to obey.

He raised his head, smiling. Then his own matter of report leaped back into his mind. Bringing his heels together, straightening up, he saluted:

"Sir, I have the honor to report that, while on the air flight, I noted the location of a solitary adobe house about four miles out. From that house came two men whom I distinctly recognized through my field glass to be Lieutenant Cantor and the bandit, Cosetta. Lieutenant Cantor, after one or two upward looks, bowed his head and kept his eyes to the ground, but I am positive, sir, of my identification of both men."

"And Cosetta's bandits?" inquired Trent. "Did you see any signs of them?"

"No, sir, but the adobe house is large enough to hide them all."

"Any trenches near the house?"

"No, sir."

"I am afraid it would do little good to approach the house in broad daylight," Lieutenant Trent reflected, excitedly, "but it should make an excellent enterprise late in the night. I will report this matter to Commander Dillingham, in command of the advanced line. With his permission, we'll try to-night for the capture of that much needed pair of rascals."

"Our signalman is being called from the advanced line, sir," reported a saluting sailorman.

Wheeling, Trent ordered his own signalman to wig-wag, "Go ahead." Then the lieutenant stood reading the message.

"You will fall back upon the advanced line," the signal read.

"Send 'O.K.,'" called the lieutenant.

"Sir," cried a sentry, "There's a party coming in. You can just make 'em out, sir."

Stepping forward, Trent brought up his fieldglasses, while Dave informed him:

"That was the second matter upon which I intended to report to you, sir. I observed those people from the airship. I believe them to be refugees."

Immediately Lieutenant Trent signaled the advanced line, reporting the party seen out on the plain.

"Then wait and escort them in," came Commander Dillingham's order.

"O.K., sir," the detachment's signalman wigwagged back.

In three-quarters of an hour more the painfully moving party reached the detachment. They were truly refugees, released from Mexico City and nearby points.

The sight of these suffering people, some hundred and twenty in number, and mainly Americans, was enough to cause many of the sailormen to shed unaccustomed tears, and not to be ashamed of them, either!

Every degree of wretchedness and raggedness was represented by these sufferers of indescribable wrongs.

Men, and women too, showed the marks of rough handling by brutal prison guards. There were many disfigured faces. One man carried in a crude sling, an arm broken by a savage Mexican captor.

Such spectacles were of daily occurrence in Vera Cruz! These wretched men, women and children had been on the way on foot since the middle of the night, having painfully trudged in over the twenty-five-mile gap in which the tracks had been torn up.

Ordering his men to fall in, Lieutenant Trent escorted the patient, footsore procession in to the advanced line. The sailormen adjusted their own steps to those of the sufferers. As they moved along Coxswain Riley vented his feelings in an undertone:

"We need only a band and a dead march to make a funeral of this! And—-yet—-no war!"

From the slow-moving ranks came only a deep, surly growl. Lieutenant Trent turned around, then faced front once more; he had no heart to utter a rebuke.

Mingled cheers and growls greeted the arrival of the pitiful fugitives at the advanced lines. The cheers were for the fact that the refugees had at least escaped with their lives. The growls were for the Mexicans responsible for this spectacle.

"We must secure conveyances of some kind to take these poor people into the city," declared Commander Dillingham. "I will send a messenger to ask for the best sort of carriages that can be found in a place like Vera Cruz. Lieutenant, as the second airship is returning yonder, your duty outside the lines is over. You may march your men to the camp yonder and let them rest until they are needed."

"I wish a word with you, sir, when possible," Trent urged.

"At once," replied Commander Dillingham. Darrin was with Lieutenant Trent when he reported the discovery of the whereabouts of Cantor and Cosetta.

"It wouldn't do any good to go out in the daytime," the commander decided. "The fellows would see you coming, and take to their heels toward the interior before you came within rifle range. You will have to go after dark, Lieutenant, and better still, towards midnight. In the early evening they might be watching for an American advance, but late at night they would decide that their hiding place is not suspected. You will plan, Lieutenant, to leave here at a little before eleven o'clock to-night, which will bring you to the adobe house about midnight. I will communicate my information to the commander of the forces ashore, and, if not reversed by him, my present instructions will hold."

The orders were not reversed. At 10.45 that night Trent marched his detachment beyond the advanced line. Every man moved as softly as he could, and there was no jingling of military accoutrements.

Finally the adobe house stood out dimly against the night sky at a distance of less than half a mile.

"If Cosetta has his men with him, they are doubtless sleeping outside, on their arms, tonight," Lieutenant Trent explained, after a softly ordered halt. "When we attack, Cantor and perhaps Cosetta, will try to escape from the rear of the house, making a quick dash for the interior, while Cosetta's men try to hold us in check. Therefore, Darrin, I am going to let you have fifteen men. You will make a wide detour of the house, and try to work to a position in the immediate rear. You will have your men lie flat on the ground, and I will take every precaution that my men do not fire upon you. If you see Cosetta or Cantor, you will know what to do."

"Aye, aye, sir," responded Ensign Darrin.

With the stealth of a cat Dave advanced, revolver in hand. He was behind the house, and within forty feet of the back door, when a crashing fire ripped out in front.

Cosetta's men, lying on the ground, had failed to note Darrin's flanking movement, but had discovered Trent's advance.

Suddenly the rear door flew open, and two men dashed out.

"Halt!" shouted Dave, dashing forward.

Cosetta reached for a revolver. Before he could produce it Darrin's bullet laid him low.

But Cantor sprang at the young ensign with such force as to bear him to earth.

One of Cantor's hands gripped at Dave's throat. In the traitor's other hand flashed a narrow-bladed Mexican knife.

"The score is settled at last!" hissed Cantor, as he drove the weapon down.

CHAPTER XXIV

CONCLUSION

It's the thought that can take shape in the hundredth part of a second that saves human life at such a crisis.

The instant he felt the hand at his throat there flashed into Dave's mind a sailor's trick that had come to him, indirectly, from Japan.

Clasping both of his own hands inside of Cantor's arm, and holding both arms rigidly, Darrin rolled himself over sideways with such force as to send the traitor sprawling.

Dave got to his feet with the speed of desperation that rules when one is in danger.

Yet the traitor was hardly a whit behind him in rising.

Crouching low, with the knife in his hand, Cantor watched his chance to spring.

Ensign Dave's revolver lay on the ground. To take the second needed to recover the weapon would cost him his life at the point of the knife.

Cosetta, lying desperately wounded, tried to crawl over the ground a few feet in order to reach his own pistol.

"Take it!" hissed Cantor, leaping forward, panther-like, and making a sudden lunge.

Throwing up his left arm to ward off the weapon, Dave felt the sharp sting of steel in his forearm.

Heedless of his wound, Dave, with his right hand, gripped the wrist of the traitor.

It was a struggle, now, of trained athletes. Each used his left hand in struggling for the advantage, watching, warily, also, for a chance to use his feet or knees.

On the other side of the house the firing still continued.

Neither Dave nor his antagonist spoke. Silently they battled, until both went to the ground.

Though Dave might have won with his fists, Cantor's superior weight and muscle counted in this deadly clinch. And now Darrin found himself lying with both shoulders touching, while Cantor, kneeling over him, fought to free his knife hand for the final thrust.

On the ground beyond, through the hail of fire from their own comrades, wriggled Riley and two sailormen. The instant they neared the corner of the house all three leaped to their feet, dashing to the aid of their young officer.

"Don't shoot, Riley!" panted Ensign Dave Darrin. "Stun him!"

In a twinkling Riley reversed his clutch on his aimed rifle, bringing down the butt across the traitor's head. Cantor rolled over.

"Shall I wind up this Greaser, sir?" asked one of the sailormen, thrusting the muzzle of his rifle against Cosetta's breast.

"No!" Dave commanded, sharply. "We don't kill when we can take prisoners."

So the seaman contented himself with standing guard over the wounded brigand.

Suddenly the machine gun began to rip into the ranks of the bandits in front of the house. An instant later a dozen sailors whom Riley had left behind reached the flanking position for which they had rushed, and began pouring in a raking fire on the bandits. Assailed from two sides Cosetta's now leaderless band broke in wild confusion, and fled, leaving behind many dead and wounded.

Quickly Trent surrounded the house, but there was no one inside.
And then Trout came upon his subordinate.

"Why, Darrin, you're hurt!" he cried, pointing to Dave's left arm.

As the firing died out Dave glanced down at his sleeve.

"Off with your blouse!" spoke the lieutenant, in a tone of command.

Riley helped to remove the blouse, meanwhile explaining:

"We didn't crawl all the way to you, sir. We ran until we got into a hail of bullets from our own messmates. Then, sir, that we might reach you, we threw ourselves down and crawled a few yards."

"Riley," declared Dave, heartily, "you're as good a man as there is in the United States Navy!"

Whereat the petty officer fairly blushed with pride.

"All our men are so good," added Trent, genially, "that it's a difficult task to pick the best."

The surviving bandits had fled. Trent's orders forbade pursuing beyond the house. So, while Riley and Dave were examining the deep wound in the latter's forearm, Trent gave orders to bury the dead in shallow graves and to pick up the wounded for removal to Vera Cruz.

Immediately upon returning to the advanced line Dave was ordered back to the "*Long Island*" for prompt surgical treatment. Though his wound was not dangerous, in itself, the climate of Vera Cruz is one in which there is the gravest danger of blood-poisoning setting in in any wound.

The day after that, duty on shore being lighter, and officers being needed aboard, Danny Grin was ordered back to ship duty, while Lieutenant Trent remained ashore with his detachment.

Having broken arrest, Cantor, on being returned to ship, was placed behind the steel bars of the ship's brig. There was no further escape for him. But his brother officers sighed their relief when a board of surgeons declared Lieutenant Cantor to be hopelessly insane, and expressed their opinion that he had been in that unfortunate mental condition for at least some weeks. That removed the taint of treason from the "*Long Island's*" ward-room, as an insane man is never held responsible for his wrong acts.

It was gambling to excess, and the fear of being dropped from the Navy Register, that had caused the wreck of Cantor's mind. He is now properly confined in an asylum.

Mrs. Black had not left Vera Cruz, but still lingered on one of the refugee ships in the harbor, where the Denmans found her. Mrs. Black was a widow who devoted her time and her wealth to missionary work in Mexico. Dave learned to his surprise that she was the daughter of Jason Denman, and a sister of the girl whom Dave had served so signally in New York.

Mr. Denman, who was a wealthy resident of an Ohio town, had extensive mining interests in Mexico, and had gone there to look after them, leaving Miss Denman and her mother in New York. Cantor, who had first met the Denmans in Ohio, when on recruiting duty in that state, had planned to make Miss Denman his wife for purely mercenary reasons. He had struggled to overcome his gaming mania, and had planned that once Miss Denman became his wife her money should be used to pay his gaming debts and free him from the claims of the vice.

But Mr. Denman, with the insight of a wise man, had discouraged the suit.

In New York, before the "*Long Island*" had sailed, Cantor had met young Tom Denman in a gambling resort. Plying the young man with liquor, Cantor had persuaded the young man, when unconscious of what he was doing, to

137

forge a banker's name to two checks, which Cantor had persuaded an acquaintance of his to cash. Of course the checks had been refused payment at the bank, but the man who had cashed them had disappeared.

Cantor had offered to save young Tom Denman. Without involving himself Cantor could have testified that the young man was all but unconscious, and without knowledge of his act, when he "forged" the cheeks.

The bank that had been deceived into cashing the checks before they were forwarded to the bank upon which they were drawn, had located Tom Denman easily enough. Tom would have been arrested, but Mrs. Denman promptly applied to a great detective agency, which quickly established the young man's mental condition at the of "forging" the checks. Moreover, Mrs. Denman, after cabling her husband for authority to use his funds, had made good the loss to the bank. Then mother, daughter and son had journeyed hastily to Vera Cruz, that the boy might be under his father's eye.

That one lesson was enough for Tom Denman. He has never strayed since.

As to the theft of his landing plan, Captain Gales afterward explained to several of his officers that no such theft had ever taken place. "You recall, gentlemen," the captain explained, "that I referred to the envelope which had contained the plans. And I then stated that the envelope which had contained the plans had disappeared. You will also remember, perhaps that I didn't state that the plans themselves were gone, for they rested in my safe, and are there at this moment. Acting that afternoon on an impulse that I did not very well understand, I took the landing plans from their envelope and filled the envelope with blank paper after having put the plans in the safe.

"Cantor had knowledge of the envelope, and supposed, as any one would have done, that the plans were inside. When my back was turned for an instant Cantor took the envelope, which I did not immediately miss, as I had no idea that any of my officers was untrustworthy. Cantor hurried to his own quarters, and there discovered the blank paper substitution. Furious, yet hating Darrin for reasons which you now understand, Cantor hastened to Darrin's room and slipped the envelope in under Darrin's mattress. Cantor has admitted it to me——whatever the word of an adjudged lunatic may be worth poor fellow!

"Now, as to Cantor's need of money, he was overwhelmed with gambling debts in New York. Some wild fancy told him that he could win money enough in Vera Cruz to pay his debts at home. He secured leave and went ashore. In a gaming house there he lost all his money, but still fought on against the game when he found that his signature would be accepted. He plunged heavily, soon rising from the table owing thirty thousand dollars to the house. Then Cosetta, who was a silent partner of the house, noting the lieutenant's despair, led him aside and cunningly informed him that he could have all his notes back if he could only secure the authoritative plans of the American landing. Cosetta, who had been a bandit for many years, and who feared the time would come when his appearance in Vera Cruz would be followed by arrest and execution, wanted to turn the landing plans over to General Maas, the Mexican commander here. Imagine the temptation to Cantor when he thought he had the plans in his own hands!

"Cantor afterwards secured my permission to go ashore in civilian garb, on the plea that he had urgent private business. As the landing had been made, I permitted him to go. I have since discovered that Cantor had word of the Denmans being in Vera Cruz. Cosetta found the family for him, and Cantor made one last, desperate plea for Miss Denman's hand. He was obliged to urge his suit through the open window of the house. Then, when Mr. Denman sternly refused to listen to him, Cosetta tried to kill Mr. Denman and his son, intending to abduct Miss Denman and to force her to marry Cantor.

"Cosetta died this morning. He had hoped to become at least a colonel in Huerta's army. Cantor did not know Cosetta until that chance meeting took place in the gambling house."

A week later, Dave Darrin, his wound now almost healed, stood on the bridge of the "Long Island," Danny Grin at his side.

They had just watched the landing of the last boatloads of General Funston's regulars.

"I believe that winds up the Navy's chapter at Vera Cruz, Danny," said Ensign Darrin. "The rest of it, if there is going to be any 'rest,' will belong to the Army."

"We had an interesting time while it lasted," declared Dalzell, with a broad grin.

"There is a world full of interesting times ahead of us. We'll find time in every quarter of the globe. Isn't that so, Gunner's Mate Riley?" he demanded of the former coxswain, who, promoted that day, now stepped upon the bridge saluting, to show proudly on his sleeve the badge of his new rating.

Whether Darrin's prediction was realized will be discovered in the pages of the next volume of this series, which will be published shortly under the title, "*Dave Darrin on Mediterranean Service; Or, With Dan Dalzell on European Duty.*"

In this forthcoming volume we shall encounter an amazing tale of an American naval officer's life and duties abroad, and we are likely, too, to hear from Lieutenant Trent and other good fellows from the ward-rooms and from the forecastles of our splendid Navy.